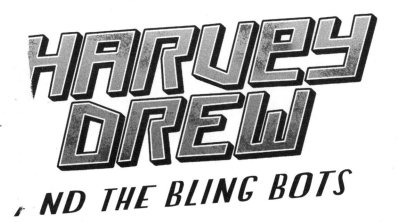

HARVEY DREW

AND THE BLING BOTS

HARVEY DREW

AND THE BLING BOTS

CAS LESTER

Illustrations by
SAM HEARN

HOT
KEY
BOOKS

First published in Great Britain in 2014 by Hot Key Books
Northburgh House, 10 Northburgh Street, London EC1V 0AT

A CIP catalogue record for this book is available from the British Library.

ISBN: 978-1-4714-0248-7

1

This book is typeset in 14pt Sabon using Atomik ePublisher

Printed and bound by Clays Ltd, St Ives Plc

FSC

Hot Key Books supports the Forest Stewardship Council (FSC),
the leading international forest certification organisation, and is
committed to printing only on Greenpeace-approved FSC-certified paper.

www.hotkeybooks.com

Hot Key Books is part of the Bonnier Publishing Group
www.bonnierpublishing.com

For Alfie, Bertie, Archie, Annie Beth and Tasha

CHAPTER ONE

Awash with litter

The *Toxic Spew* is the grottiest, grubbiest spaceship in Galaxy 43b. Frankly, everybody in the entire Known Universe, and Beyond knows that it's a disgustingly filthy, tatty old pile of junk.

If you sat in the shabby black captain's chair in the middle of the command bridge you'd be gobsmacked by the state of the place. It's awash with litter – empty pizza boxes, crushed drinks cartons and sweet wrappers. And you'd be pretty careful where you put your hands because the control desks are covered with horrible sticky black grime.

The deck is so slimy with dregs of spilt drinks and slops of tomato sauce that the crew's space boots stick to it and make a slurpy, sucky noise as they walk along.

The stench of rotting rubbish is so gross I'm not even going to describe it because it'd make your eyes water so much you wouldn't be able to read.

You would think the captain would do something about it, wouldn't you?

But then you're from Earth, aren't you? And I don't want to be rude, but hey, what do you know?

Which explains why, as this story starts (on Novaday the 92nd of Luna), the crew are sitting round the command bridge having a galaxy-class whinge.

Squabbling on the command bridge

'It's all so tedious,' groaned Senior Engineering Officer Gizmo clutching at his short

multicoloured hair. 'Emptying countless tubs of toilet waste from pangalactic starships or scooping up tons of rocket trash or toxic gloop from the HyperspaceWays.'

'And it's so pointless,' moaned Pilot Officer Maxie sitting with her elbows on the flight desk, her purple face cupped in her hands. 'I mean as soon as we suck up . . .'

'*Vacuum* up!' corrected Scrummage. As Chief Rubbish Officer he was very touchy about the ship's garbage kit. Not so touchy that he didn't mind putting his filthy space boots up on the garbage control desk.

Maxie shot him a withering look with her bright turquoise eyes and carried on. 'As soon as we *suck up* one pool of revolting toxic gloop then an even more disgusting one drifts in from somewhere else.'

Scrummage leant back in his seat, his scruffy multicoloured ponytail hanging limply from his balding head. He raised one white eyebrow and said . . .

(Hang on. You did notice that the crew have purple faces and multicoloured hair, white eyebrows and turquoise eyes, didn't you? And you've probably even worked out they're not from Earth.

But I bet you didn't know they're from the planet Zeryx Minor, did you, Smartypants?

It's not your fault of course. You don't study 'The A–Z of Intergalactic Life Forms' in Earth schools, do you? And I bet you can't even download it from the Outernet.

You must feel horribly left out in your remote corner of the universe.)

'Look, it might not be the most glamorous job', said Scrummage. 'But . . .'

'Glamorous? It's ghastly!' Gizmo butted in, sneering down his rather hooked nose.

'As Chief Rubbish Officer, may I point out that space junk is a serious danger to interplanetary traffic. We do a vital job.'

'No, we do a rubbish job . . . and *you* are a Rubbish Officer.'

Maxie laughed.

Fight, fight, fight!

'Gentlemen!' said Harvey in a warning tone. Scrummage and Gizmo were heading for a spat and he wanted to nip it in the bud.

'It's daring and dangerous!' exclaimed Scrummage.

It's disgusting and dirty,' sniffed Gizmo. 'It's also, revolting and repulsive, gruesome and gross. Like you.'

Scrummage swung his legs angrily off the control desk and hitched up his filthy green and yellow overalls over his vast belly. 'Right! That's it!' he snorted, storming over to Gizmo.

'Fight, fight, fight!' chanted Maxie.

CHAPTER TWO

No brawling on the bridge!

Harvey leapt out of his seat and jumped in between Scrummage and Gizmo before they started slugging it out with their bare fists.

It might be helpful if I mention that although Harvey doesn't have much experience as a spaceship captain (almost none in fact) he was captain of the Highford All Stars football team back home on Earth for two seasons running.

Obviously, his teammates weren't anything like as stroppy as the crew of the *Toxic Spew*. And he hadn't actually had to face many literally deadly dangerous and fatally lethal situations on the pitch (like poisonous killer maggots, a multiple spacecraft pile-up and exploding garbage). But he's a quick learner.

And, of course, the crew think the Highford All Stars is a spaceship. And he hasn't *quite* got round to telling them it's actually a football team.

> *(Look, I don't want to give you the wrong idea about Harvey. He's not deliberately lying. It's just that tactically there hasn't been a good moment to . . . er . . . fess up.)*

'No brawling on the bridge,' ordered Harvey, pushing Scrummage and Gizmo apart. 'And, Maxie, what kind of behaviour is that, encouraging a fight?'

'Spoilsport,' said Maxie.

'He started it!' said Scrummage, prodding his finger at Gizmo.

'No you did!'

'Pack it in!' ordered Harvey.

'"Pack it in!"? What kind of order is that?

From a spaceship commander?' laughed Maxie.

Harvey sighed. She never missed a chance to get a dig in. Maxie wasn't much older than him, or much bigger. She had to roll the sleeves and legs of her uniform up to stop them flapping around. But she was a brilliant pilot. And she didn't like being bossed around by anyone. Let alone an eleven-year-old boy from a planet they'd never even heard of and couldn't even find on a 3D digital star map.

Fortunately for Harvey, the crew were suddenly distracted.

Rocket Fuel Special

SCHWOOOSH!

The doors to the bridge opened and Medical Officer Yargal slurped onto the bridge, her three yellow eyes waggling on their stalks. She oozed across the deck, like a large green slug, her huge single slimy foot trailing sticky grey slime in its wake. A pile of pizza boxes and drinks cartons slithered around alarmingly in her six slippery blue tentacles. Strings of gunk dribbled down onto the boxes making them soggy.

(The one snag of having a Yargillian as Medical Officer and Ship's Cook is that the constant dribbling and oozing can put you off your lunch. Yargillians are one of the most revolting life forms in the entire Known Universe, and Beyond – but it isn't polite to mention it, obviously.)

Snuffles, the ship's dog, lolloped behind her, looking like a cross between a hungry Grey Wolf and an even hungrier Great White Shark – vast, shaggy, slobbery and utterly terrifying.

'Lunch!' cried Yargal.

Everyone grabbed the boxes greedily. Snuffles settled himself at Harvey's feet, dribbling hopefully. Strings of saliva slobbered off his massive teeth and dripped onto the grimy deck.

DRIBBLE, DRIBBLE! DROOL, DROOL!

'Do we have to have a Hazard Hunting Hound from Canine Major on the bridge at lunchtime?' challenged Maxie.

Since nobody *ever* cleaned anything up on the *Toxic Spew,* Harvey had thought they might as well let the dog slobber up some of the muck. Of course the bridge wasn't exactly spotless – but it was better than it had been. You could actually see the floor in places.

So he ignored Maxie, and patted Snuffles on the head, who gave him a friendly nudge with his raw meatball of a nose. He really was a lovely hound, once you got over: your fear, his teeth . . . and the drool.

Harvey opened his pizza box and froze in horror.

'It's my Rocket Fuel Special,' boasted Yargal. 'Pilchards in pineapple jelly with molten mozzarella and extra hot spicy sauce with a secret ingredient!' She winked at Harvey with the middle one of her three yellow waggly eyes.

Harvey had got used to the Yargillian's repulsive looks. But he would never get used to her repulsive pizza 'Specials'. This one was topped with an alarming lime green sauce, which probably glowed in the dark.

'Er . . . could I just have a plain cheese and tomato one?' he said, remembering the crunchy deep-pan ones his mum used to buy and how he dunked the crusts in a dollop of ketchup and mayo mixed. He sighed. The crew had promised they would get him home one day and to the *exact* same time and place he'd left, so that *technically* his family wouldn't miss him at all. But that didn't stop him missing his family.

Molten mozzarella!

'Oh, come on, Captain,' spat Scrummage with his mouthful of food. 'Be adventurous!' Greedily he tore off another slice of his cheese, chocolate banana custard and chilli sauce pizza and rammed it in his mouth. A large blob of greasy gooey mozzarella slid down between the switches on the garbage desk in front of him.

'Mind the controls!' snapped Gizmo.

'Don't fuss!' snorted Scrummage, prodding at the blob of molten cheese with his grubby fingers and shoving it down between the switches. 'It's only the smallest mini, micro, milli-atom of molten mozzarella.'

There was a nasty buzzing sound,

BZZZZ BZZ BZZZZZZ FFZZZZZ

exactly as if some electrical wires were touching each other when they shouldn't be, and then:

KA-BOOM!

WHOOOOMPH!

There was a small explosion and a shower of sparks as the garbage control panel caught fire.

CHAPTER THREE

Fire!

'Multicoloured chunder!' yelped Scrummage, leaping back from his desk as flames flickered round the controls.

DRRIIIIIING!

WHOOP! WHOOP! WHOOP!

The ship's alarms screamed and warning lights flashed sickeningly yellow around the command bridge.

Snuffles yelped and starting howling.

AROOOO, AROUOUOU, AROOO!

The computer's digital voice broke through with frankly irritating cheerfulness. 'I hate to alarm you, Captain, but could I just draw your attention to the fact that there is, unless I am very much mistaken, a fire on the bridge?'

But Harvey had already grabbed the fire extinguisher.

'Fire on the bridge!' screamed Yargal, waggling her tentacles hysterically and getting in his way. 'Captain, save me! I'm too young to die in a fire on the bridge.'

(That's the one snag of having a Yargillian on your crew. They do tend to over-react in a crisis.)

DRRIIIIIING!

WHOOP! WHOOP! WHOOP!

AROOOO, AROUOUOU, AROOO!

Harvey doubted anything as damp and slimy as Yargal could actually catch fire. He aimed the fire extinguisher at the flames.

WHOOOOOOSH!

A stream of bright pink foam smothered the garbage control desk like a giant marshmallow. Maxie, sitting no more than a metre away at the flight desk carried on casually eating her pizza and wafting the worst of the smoke and steam away.

DRRIIIIIING!

WHOOP! WHOOP! WHOOP!

went the alarms.

AROOOO, AROUOUOU, AROOO!

went Snuffles.

'Snuffles, quiet!' ordered Harvey. 'And

computer, cut alarms.'

'Do you mean: "Computer, cut alarms *please?*"' said the computer snippily.

'Sorry, yes. Computer, cut alarms *please.*'

'Thank you! Just because there's a little bit of a panic on the bridge, doesn't mean we have to forget our manners.' It bleeped off huffily and cut the alarms.

DRRIIIII . . .

WHOO . . .

(Sorry, I'm not sure how to spell sounds that get cut off, but you get the idea.)

Again, no brawling on the bridge!

Gizmo threw down his pizza slice and stormed over to the garbage control desk. 'Not again! Captain, may I remind you of the Intergalactic Travel and Transport Pact rules and regulations regarding keeping critical controls clean?' he cried.

Scrummage leapt to his feet and spitting pizza crumbs over Gizmo's spotless overalls said, 'That's your job! You're the Engineering Officer.'

'How dare you! You eat like a giant space hog from the Nova Pigasus Nebula!'

Scrummage pointed a large slice of pizza threateningly at Gizmo. 'Don't you make personal remarks about me,' he spluttered.

Maxie tucked her hair behind her ears, leant her elbows on the flight desk and grinned at her fellow officers.

Snuffles dribbled hopefully. There was every chance Gizmo and Scrummage would lose their tempers and start throwing large chunks of pizza around. Frankly, there was every chance Gizmo and Scrummage would start throwing each other around.

'Gentlemen. May I remind you of *my* rules and regulations regarding brawling on the bridge?' said Harvey firmly.

A few moments of peace and calm returned to the bridge.

Until Harvey took a large bite out of his Rocket Fuel Special pizza and . . . screamed.

'AAAAAAAARGH!'

CHAPTER FOUR

Death by pizza

Harvey choked, his eyes and nose streaming violently. Yargal's Rocket Fuel Special with its bright green glow-in the-dark extra hot spicy sauce had nearly blown his head off.

Yargal thumped him on the back with a slimy tentacle. 'Sorry, sir. Was it a bit spicy for you?'

'What did you put in it?' he gasped.

'I told you – pilchards, pineapple jelly, mozzarella and extra hot spicy sauce . . . with just a hint of rocket fuel.'

'Rocket fuel! You actually put *rocket fuel* in the sauce? I thought that was just a nickname.'

(That's the one snag of having a Yargillian as Medical Officer and Ship's Cook. They can eat pretty much anything (even boiled Brussels sprouts) and they don't know that you humans are quite, er . . . picky eaters.

Especially when it comes to eating food that can actually, literally and painfully melt your tonsils.)

'Yargal! You could have killed me!'

Maxie burst out laughing. 'Death by pizza! Not a very *heroic* way to die!'

Harvey lay under the water cooler at the back of the bridge with his mouth wide open and turned the tap on FULL. Water poured down his throat, splashed all over his face and splattered onto the deck. Snuffles stood over him trying to catch the drips with his huge rubbery tongue. It wasn't a very impressive position for a spaceship captain to be in. Maxie rolled her eyes.

'I'll take command if you're not well, Captain,' said Gizmo, heading for the captain's chair in the centre of the bridge.

'NO!' snapped Maxie and Scrummage, and Gizmo reluctantly sat back down.

'I'm sorry, Captain,' said Yargal sadly and squelched damply off the bridge, taking Snuffles with her.

Speckled vomit!

The lights on the computer's console flickered busily and it bleeped importantly.

'Captain, I hate to interrupt you because:

a) it's rude

and

b) you are obviously very busy taking a shower . . .

'Oh, by the way, can I just mention that we have a fully functional bathroom on the ship with hot and cold running water, a soap dispenser and a plug on a bit of string?

'Anyhow, I'm picking up an urgent distress signal from a SupaCosmicCargo ship in the

Gamma Delton XL Belt.' It paused for effect, then added: 'It's carrying a cargo of Techno-tium.'

'Techno-tium? TECHNO-TIUM!' cried Scrummage. 'Speckled vomit!'

CHAPTER FIVE

Chaos on the bridge

They couldn't believe their luck. In all their multiple intergalactic missions, the Bin Men of the *Toxic Spew* had never, ever found any Techno-tium. Not even a tiny little nanocrumb.

'Yahoooo!' they cried.

Harvey was stunned to see the entire bridge crew whooping and cheering and leaping up and down.

(I don't like to be rude, but you don't have anything nearly as advanced as Techno-tium on your funny little planet, do you?

*It's the strongest metal in the entire Known
Universe, and Beyond. It's bendier than rubber,
stretchier than elastic and lighter than air. Imagine
a large solid lump of metal, floating like a helium-
filled balloon.*

*Of course it does tend to drift off far, far away
into outer space, which can be tricky if you're
holding onto a large chunk of it and you've
forgotten to tie it down.*

*Particularly since you won't ever want to let
go of it because . . . it's also the most valuable
metal in the entire Known Universe, and Beyond.)*

After a few minutes of mayhem and madness,
the crew calmed down enough to notice that
Harvey was sitting in the tatty black captain's
chair utterly bewildered.

Hmmm, tricky sums

'Captain,' said Gizmo. 'May I remind you of
the Intergalactic Travel and Transport Pact rules
and regulations regarding rescuing cargo ships?

'Er . . . yes please,' said Harvey, who had absolutely no idea what they were.

'Basically, if we rescue a cargo freighter, we get the cargo as our fee!'

'Multicoloured upchuck!' cried Scrummage, his turquoise eyes shining with greed. 'We're rich!'

'How much is the cargo worth?' asked Harvey.

'No idea,' grinned Scrummage, rubbing his hands greedily.

So Harvey asked the computer.

'Hmmm,' it said importantly. 'Tricky.'

'It depends on:

    a) how much Techno-tium there is
    b) how many zeros there are in a gazillion and
    c) where that funny little decimal dot goes.'

Its lights flickered furiously. 'But I'm pretty sure that a nanocrumb of pure Techno-tium is worth – ooh lots!'

'Thank you,' said Harvey, with a hint of sarcasm.

'My pleasure,' said the computer brightly and bleeped off.

'Who cares exactly what it's worth!' spluttered Scrummage. 'It'll be a fortune!'

'Come on, Captain, let's go!' cried Maxie, sitting poised at the flight control desk waiting for Harvey's orders.

Hmmm, tricky questions

But Harvey was wary. He hadn't known his Chief Rubbish Officer very long, but he knew he could be reckless. And that he'd happily load all sorts of horrendously hazardous garbage onto the *Toxic Spew*, if it were worth enough cosmic cash. So he grilled his Rubbish Officer closely.

'Is it dangerous?'

'Nope.'

'Poisonous?'

'Nope.'

'Illegal?'

'Nope.'

'Explosive?'

'Nope.'

'Is it repulsive, disgusting, revolting, rotting, putrid or in any way likely to make the entire crew vomit themselves to death?'

'Nope! It's not even smelly. Just very, very valuable.'

'So what are we waiting for, Captain?' Maxie drummed her fingers on the flight desk. 'If we don't get going someone else will there first and snaffle it.

'And we'll miss out the chance of a lifetime and have to spend the rest of our pitiful lives on the *Toxic Spew* collecting endless amounts of repulsive rubbish until we all die a hideous death by a catching a fatal dose of Festering Garbage Pox!'

Hmmm, tricky decision

'Maxie's right, Captain,' said Gizmo. 'And may I point out that if we get a cargo of Technotium we'll be rich enough to stop garbage collection and concentrate on looking for your planet Earth and get you home.'

Harvey hadn't thought of that. But now that Gizmo mentioned it, he had to admit that although he was having the greatest adventure in the galaxy, he was really beginning to miss home, his mates, his mum and dad, and football – especially football.

'OK, fine,' he said. 'Computer, tell the SupaCosmicCargo ship we're on our way and plot a course for the Gamma thingy whatsit Belt.'

'Did I hear a *please*?' snipped the computer.

'OK, please!' said Harvey. Blimey, the computer was in a really stroppy mood today.

Eagerly Maxie slid the flight joysticks forward to Cosmic Speed 8 and Harvey felt the familiar

LURCH

as he was flung backwards in his seat as the little intergalactic garbage ship hurtled forward into hyperspace. Then he felt the familiar

THWACK

as the back of his head slapped against the metal headrest of his seat.

The planets and stars on the vast vision screens on all three sides of the bridge seemed to shimmer and then whoosh backwards as the ship zoomed off through the cosmos.

The gobsmacking awesomeness of outer space

Harvey sat back to enjoy the ride. He was never, ever going to get used to the thrill of space flight – not even if he lived to be a hundred and six. It was . . .

AMAZING

ASTONISHING

and

ASTOUNDING!

(You might be interested to know that although Galaxy 43b is a fairly scruffy corner of the universe, some bits are actually quite stunning. But then again you might not be. In which case you can just skip the next bit.)

The four moons of the Bebinca Flummery Belt are particularly spectacular. They constantly shimmer and change from bright blue through turquoise to pale green and back again.

ZOOM ...

The *Toxic Spew* rocketed past them so quickly they didn't even have time to change from green back to turquoise.

WHIZZ ...

It zipped around the massive deep purple planet PannaCotta with its seven swirling bands of orange toxic gas. And then ...

WHOOOSH ...

It shot through the dazzlingly bright multicoloured shooting stars of the Semolina Cluster.

It's like flying through an enormous firework display, thought Harvey, gobsmacked. This is ... OUT OF THIS WORLD!

(And of course he's right. Well, it's out of your world anyhow. In fact, come to think of it, it's out of your Galaxy!)

So the *Toxic Spew* bravely raced to the rescue of the SupaCosmicCargo craft and its crew. And its gobsmackingly valuable payload of course.

Then, all they'd have to do is tow the ship to an interstellar scrapyard and claim the cargo.

What could possibly go wrong?

Believe me, you don't want to know.

CHAPTER SIX

Toxic Spew to the rescue

As the *Toxic Spew* zipped silently across Galaxy 43b, the bridge crew thought about what they'd do with all the cosmic cash they would have once they'd sold the Techno-tium. They'd be rich!

'I'd buy the new Cygnus 7 single-seater shuttle craft with its revolutionary TripTronic gearing system,' said Senior Engineering Officer Gizmo longingly.

'Cool,' nodded Pilot Officer Maxie at the flight controls.

'I'd have a personal 3D pizza printer and

unlimited supplies of mozzarella, chocolate, banana custard and chilli sauce,' said Rubbish Officer Scrummage greedily.

'Oh, gross!' laughed Maxie. 'I'd go for a Cassini Personal HeliDroid, with inbuilt VidiScape gaming system, subsonic sound, 3V-360 VisionVisor, multi-player, multi-platform and multi-universe enabled features, downloadable cosmic content capability, pangalactic performance power enhancers and the Stella BonusBox.' Then, finally stopping to breathe, she added, 'What about you, Captain?'

'I'd buy Manchester United,' said Harvey wistfully.

The bridge crew exchanged puzzled looks and Maxie was just about to ask Harvey what a 'Manchester United' was when the computer cut in.

'Oh, don't ask me then!' it blurted out emotionally. 'Don't bother to include me in the game.'

'Sorry,' said Harvey, who hadn't realised the computer wanted to join in. 'Er . . . what would you like?'

'Not saying,' snipped the computer:
 a) you're just being polite
 b) you're not really interested
    and
 c) it's too late.'
And it bleeped off in a huff.

Spaceship ahead

Zooming through outer space at Cosmic Speed 8 the *Toxic Spew* didn't take long to get to the broken-down cargo ship.

Harvey's eyes were glued to the front vision screen ahead. He had loads of model spaceships and UFOs pinned to his bedroom ceiling back home, but he wanted to see what a real cargo spaceship would actually look like.

Eventually he saw it looming up ahead. It appeared to be a Day-Glo yellow round, flat disc with a domed middle.

'It's a flying saucer!'

'Er, no,' said Gizmo confused. 'It's a SupaCosmicCargo ship. Well, technically that bit's the freight container. The cargo ship itself is a tiny little tug on the other side.'

It's hard to get an idea of size in outer space. Because there isn't anything bobbing around to give you a sense of scale, like say, a Blue Whale or an ice cream van or a small clear plastic ruler.

Harvey had seen the cargo ship from a distance – about two thousand cosmic kilometres to be precise – and so the cargo freighter looked very small. But as the *Toxic Spew* flew nearer and nearer he saw it was huge, improbably huge.

(You might like to know that technically it wasn't 'Huge' – it was 'Quite Large'.

For a spaceship to be classed as 'Huge' by the Intergalactic Travel and Transport Pact it has to be 500 metres long, 300 metres wide and 100 metres high, and have shops, a skating rink, burger and pizza takeaways and a 3V holo-screen cinema with Q4 sound and three kinds of popcorn.

The pangalactic holiday cruisers from the Gallobium Galaxy are so massive you have to catch a bus to get from the command bridge to the loo.)

Maxie hauled back the flight controls, flicked a few switches and set the *Toxic Spew* to auto-orbit. As they rounded the giant Day-Glo yellow container they could see the SupaCosmicCargo ship itself. It was a tiny little tug, way smaller than the *Toxic Spew*.

It might be tiny, but it was the coolest thing Harvey had ever seen.

Rocket science

The model spaceships that hung from Harvey's bedroom ceiling were complicated shapes with lots of sticky out bits and added-on details in an effort to make them look real.

But this ship was totally smooth on the outside

and was basically just a triangle with a point at the front. The two side points of the triangle were bent up at the ends and looked a bit like wings.

It was completely flat on the underside, but the top was domed and, wrapped around the front and sides at the very top, was a huge vision screen.

It was sleek, it was simple, it was awesome.

And also, improbably tiny.

It didn't seem possible to Harvey that such a small ship could tow something so vast.

(But then he's new to the job so he probably doesn't understand the laws of friction in space travel. And I bet you don't either.

Look, if you don't like maths you can miss out the next bit. But if everyone on Earth does that, then how will your tiny little planet ever get to grips with interstellar space travel? I'll make it simple and please at least try to understand:

Push + Friction = Slow, Slow, Slow . . . Stop

Push – Friction = Go, Go, Go . . . Go

Now concentrate, because this bit is critical:

There is no friction in space. So once you give something a shove, it just keeps on going.

See – it's not that tricky, is it? It's hardly rocket science. Oh hang on, yes it is.)

Harvey ordered the computer to contact the cargo ship. Actually, he had to ask very nicely since the computer was in such a stroppy mood.

Intergalactic GarbleTranslate

'Go ahead, Captain,' said the computer. 'Ship-to-ship SpaceTime is connected and I have taken the liberty of turning on Intergalactic GarbleTranslate so you can understand each other.'

'Thank you,' said Harvey calmly, but his mind had suddenly gone a complete blank. He'd never done this before. But of course he didn't want the crew to know that. What on earth, or rather what in Galaxy 43b, was he actually supposed to say?

Gizmo gave an embarrassed cough, Scrummage mouthed 'Come on' and Maxie rolled her eyes.

As captain of the All Stars it'd been Harvey's job to talk to the referee, and sometimes in some pretty awkward situations. And he'd always done pretty well at it – he had a knack of being polite and sticking to the point. So he pulled himself together and said confidently: 'This is Captain Harvey Drew, Commander of the Intergalactic Garbage Ship the *Toxic Spew*. How can we help you?'

Intergalactic garble

There was a beat of silence then a thin, crisp voice said:

'The SupaCosmicCargo Delivery Company thanks you for your prompt response. Our shields are down and you may transport aboard. Please note this Special Offer ends in five minutes and be advised the SupaCosmicCargo

Delivery Company accepts no responsibility for visitors. Terms and conditions apply. Always read the small print.'

'Er, thank you,' said Harvey.

Gizmo strode purposefully over to the captain's chair. 'Assuming command in your absence, Captain,' he said pompously.

Scrummage had left his post at the garbage control desk and was standing by, itching to transport aboard. 'Well come on, Captain!'

Standby, Captain!

'Right,' said Harvey, going to stand next to him. 'Computer, I'd be grateful if you could transport Officer Scrummage and me onto the SupaCosmicCargo ship.'

'With pleasure!' replied the computer sweetly.

'Oh please!' snorted Maxie. 'Fine captain you're turning out to be. Can't even order the ship's computer around!'

But Harvey knew the computer could be a

bit careless at transporting. So he didn't want
to risk upsetting it.

There was an irritatingly high whining noise
that made Harvey wince and he braced himself.

SKREEE-E-E-EEEEH!

'Standby, Captain!' yelled Scrummage above
the noise. 'Oh, by the way, they're Zinians from
the planet X-Zin cum Delta, so for goodness'
sake try not to over-react.' (Harvey had fainted,
actually fainted, the first time he ever saw
Yargal. And the astounded crew would never
let him forget it.)

The command bridge of the *Toxic Spew*
wobbled and then sort of melted around them . . .
and they found themselves looking at the
command bridge of the SupaCosmicCargo ship.

But from the outside of the ship!

'AAAAAAAARGH!' screamed Harvey and
Scrummage.

CHAPTER SEVEN

Oooops!

Harvey and Scrummage clung onto the massive front vision screen wipers of the SupaCosmicCargo ship for dear life.

'HEEEEEEELP!' they screamed.

Harvey's mind flooded with fear and questions. *How were they going to get into the spaceship? How long could they survive without air? And what if the Zinians turned the screen wipers on?*

Fighting back panic he turned to Scrummage

and saw his eyes were wide open in terror, but he had clamped his mouth shut. So Harvey shut his mouth and concentrated on keeping the precious air he did have in his lungs er . . . inside his lungs.

He forced himself to let go of the wiper with one hand and used it to hammer frantically on the plasti-glass screen. Scrummage copied him.

THUMP-THUMP-THUMP!

BANG-BANG-BANG!

Dying to breathe

Harvey was desperate to breathe in. He felt his eyes glazing over and he began to see stars (no not real stars, the ones you see when you're out of oxygen and about to pass out.)

Through the vision screen they could see two tall, slim Zinians.

Harvey battled back the urge to shout:

'HELP!'

knowing that it would be the last word he ever uttered. Keeping his mouth clamped tight he went:

'MMMMMMMMMMMMMM!'

and pounded even more feverishly:

THUMP-THUMP-THUMP-THUMP-THUMP!

BANG-BANG-BANG-BANG-BANG!

Finally, the Zinians glanced up. They were slightly surprised to find their visitors on the outside. But they were fully trained interplanetary cargo couriers and nothing shocked them. Within seconds they had efficiently transported Harvey and Scrummage safely inside.

Phew!

Harvey crouched doubled-up on the floor, panting hard and suffering the worst stitch cramps ever. Scrummage was collapsed in a heap nearby. Frantically and thankfully they gulped down cool oxygen from the ship's air conditioning system.

But since Harvey was match fit it didn't take him long to recover and start looking around. He was a bit surprised to find they were in a small cool cubicle with gleaming white walls and no obvious door.

'What the . . .?' he started to say, but was cut off when –

SPLOOOOOOSH!

He and Scrummage were suddenly and completely drenched head to foot by a powerful jet spray of water – fresh pine, but with a hint of lemon and lime.

'What the . . .?' Harvey tried again, but was

cut off again as . . .

WHOOOOOOOOSH!

They were blasted by gale-force hot air. It was like being blow dried by hurricane.

When they were completely dry it stopped. Scrummage's uniform, which was usually utterly filthy, was now completely spotless and freshly laundered. And his multicoloured ponytail that usually hung limp and greasy at the back of his balding head, looked immaculate.

Scrummage took one look at Harvey and burst out laughing. Every strand of Harvey's bright red curly hair was standing on end. He looked ridiculous.

'Sorry, Captain,' laughed Scrummage, 'I should have warned you the Zinians are a bit fussy about hygiene!'

SupaCosmic clean

Before Harvey could reply, the white doors of the shower unit slid back to reveal a brilliantly lit corridor with shiny white walls and floor, and a remote voice said:

'The SupaCosmicCargo Delivery Company welcomes you aboard this SupaCosmicCargo ship. Please make your way to the bridge by following the blue direction arrows on the floor. The SupaCosmicCargo Delivery Company accepts no responsibility for you during your visit. Thank you.'

Stepping out of the cubicle they followed the line of arrows along the squeaky-clean walkway. Harvey doing his best to smarm his hair down as they went. Peering through a spotlessly clean plasti-glass door on the right, Harvey saw an astonishingly clean galley lined with galaxy-class computerised cooking equipment. The only thing he recognised was a stack of white poly cups and some plastic-looking cutlery (all white, obviously). There was something that looked a bit like a microwave but with computerised controls and a joystick! *Blimey!* thought Harvey, *that takes playing with your food to a whole new level!*

A bit further along he glanced through another plasti-glass door at the sleeping quarters. They were utterly spotless with pure white walls and floors and white bunks with white covers. It was hard to make out where the walls started and the floors finished. Harvey was beginning to think the Zinians were overdoing the white theme a bit.

SupaCosmic cool

The last door on the left was labelled: Playroom. *Playroom?!* thought Harvey. He looked in. It was completely empty, except for a small white remote control device and a visor on the floor.

(Sorry to break into the tour of the Zinian ship – but you have absolutely no idea what Harvey's looking at, do you?

Actually I've just realised, those of you who were concentrating at the beginning of Chapter Six, might just guess.

It's a VidiScapeRoom – only one of the coolest things in the entire Known Universe, and Beyond!

Now, I know you do have some (actually pretty primitive) virtual reality games on your little planet – but believe me this is AWESOME.

You can invent and play out any scenario you want – anything and anywhere – just by using your imagination!

Cool or what!? I bet you can't wait for gaming on your world to catch up.)

Harvey moved on. He suddenly realised he couldn't smell anything – except improbably fresh air. The 'air' on the *Toxic Spew* is disgustingly smelly and stale. It tastes like it's been breathed in and out thousands of times already. Which . . . er . . . it has of course. But the air on this ship smelled as fresh as the kind you get on a cold, crisp snowy day. And the ship was almost totally silent, except for a gentle busy humming sound and the clunking of their feet on the metallic floor.

Harvey was impressed.

SupaCosmic class

The SupaCosmicCargo ship is tiny, so it only took a few moments to reach the bridge. The doors slid open silently to reveal two Zinians seated at the flight desk.

Harvey was gobsmacked.

(Since you're from Earth I'm guessing you've never met Zinians from the planet X-Zin cum Delta.

So to help you picture the scene, Zinians are basically humanoid, basically blue and basically ... um, and I'm trying to find a polite way of saying this ... pointy with rather sharp edges.

Their smart blue SupaCosmicCargo Delivery

Company uniforms have sharp shoulder pads, which make their entire upper bodies er . . . triangular.)

To be fair to Harvey, he was less gobsmacked by the sight of two bright blue triangular aliens than he was by the sight of the command bridge itself.

Banks of monitors and switches, buttons and levers covered every wall. And everything was sleek, shiny and squeaky clean. Oh, and, you've guessed it: white!

It was impressive.

It was classy.

It was everything the *Toxic Spew* wasn't.

One of the Zinians stood up smartly. 'The SupaCosmicCargo Delivery Company is happy to hand over responsibility for the cargo instantly,' he said.

'Thank you!' said Scrummage. 'Um, do you happen to know how much Techno-tium there is?' he asked casually.

'Negative,' replied the Zinian. 'The SupaCosmicCargo Delivery Company is not responsible for:

the quantity,

the colour,

the existence of the cargo.

Or feeding, watering or exercising the cargo.'

Briskly he handed Harvey a smart white digipad and a cool white metal stylo. 'The SupaCosmicCargo Delivery Company requests you sign here to take responsibility for the cargo.'

'Glittering upchuck!'

Harvey signed.

A new page instantly scrolled up.

'Sign here to take responsibility of the freight container.' Harvey did so . . . and then carried on signing for what seemed to be about ten minutes . . .

'Sign here to say you are not insane.

'Here to enter the prize drawer to win a holiday on X-Zin cum Delta (off-peak season only).

'Here to say you've read our terms and conditions.'

'Er . . . should I just read them?' asked Harvey.

The Zinian gave him a sharp look. 'Nobody ever reads them – they only sign to say that they have. They're 148 pages long and no pictures.'

Harvey signed and the Zinian carried on.

'Sign here to say you are happy to get our advertising SpaceMails.

'Here to say you are over 18.'

'But I'm not,' said Harvey.

'You don't have to be,' said the Zinian. 'You only have to say that you are.'

'Er . . . OK,' said Harvey, signing.

'And finally sign here and select your home planet from the drop-down menu.'

Harvey signed and then scrolled down the list of planets. 'Ah,' he said.

The Zinian raised a sharp angled eyebrow. 'Problem?'

'My planet isn't on the list.'

The Zinians gasped.

'Glittering upchuck!' Scrummage nearly exploded with frustration.

CHAPTER EIGHT

Bad news

The Zinian turned to his crewmate. 'Can we hand over the cargo to an alien from a non-listed planet?'

'Negative.'

'Ah,' said the Zinian and put his hand out for the digipad.

Scrummage was desperate. 'Can't he just leave that bit?' he begged.

'Negative. The SupaCosmicCargo Delivery Company demands forms are completed in full.'

'Can't we put *my* planet?' said Scrummage.

For a few agonising seconds the Zinian

considered this bold suggestion and Scrummage literally held his breath.

Eventually the Zinian said: 'Fine.'

Scrummage breathed out, selected 'Zeryx Minor' and the Zinian took the digipad back.

'The SupaCosmicCargo Delivery Company thanks you for your business. Terms and conditions apply. Always read the small print. Goodbye,' he said and turned back to the flight desk.

Scrummage hitched his filthy overalls up excitedly. 'Captain, we are now the proud, and very wealthy owners of a cargo of Techno-tium!' he said. 'Let's go!'

More bad news

Seconds later Harvey and Scrummage were safely back on the command bridge of the *Toxic Spew*. They were just in time to watch the Zinian tug ship unclip its tow bar from the container. Then there was a small flare as it powered its subatomic reactor launchers and very slowly drifted off into the blackness of deep space, leaving the flying saucer, sorry, cargo container, just hanging there.

'Hang on,' said Harvey. 'What about the crew?'

'Who cares?' said Scrummage.

'I do!'

'That's very noble of you, Captain,' said Officer Gizmo. 'But the SupaCosmicCargo Delivery Company will send a ship to recover the space-tug and crew.'

'So why didn't they just wait? Why did they put out a distress signal and hand the cargo over to us?'

'Because it's dangerous to be hanging around with a cargo container full of Techno-tium,' said Scrummage.

'I thought you said the cargo wasn't dangerous?' cried Harvey, horrified.

'It isn't. It's valuable,' explained Gizmo. 'It's having a valuable cargo that's dangerous.'

'How dangerous?'

Scrummage shrugged.

'Very,' grinned Maxie.

(You don't get a lot of space pirates, in your quiet little corner of the universe, do you?

Lucky, lucky you.

Ruthless and rich with the fastest ships in the universe, they're a complete menace.

Technically they're banned under the Intergalactic Travel and Transport Pact rules and regulations regarding behaving nicely.

But outer space is so massive it's almost lawless in some places.

There's the Intergalactic Traffic Police of course. But there are only six ships for about a gazillion square light years of open space so . . . you do the sums.)

Even more bad news

Maxie tucked her hair behind her ears, leant her elbows on the flight desk and said casually,

'Oh yes, in this part of Galaxy 43b there's stacks of murderous space pirates and cosmic corsairs. And they'd stop at nothing to get their hands on some Techno-tium.

'And I mean literally nothing – they'll tear us limb from limb, gouge out our eyes, slit our throats, rip out our gizzards and poison our pizza.

'And if that doesn't work, they'll just kill us and take it anyway,' she finished helpfully.

CHAPTER NINE

A magnet for danger

Seeing the horrified look on Harvey's face, Maxie burst out laughing. 'Relax! Who's going to think a grotty little intergalactic garbage ship like the *Toxic Spew* has anything worth taking?'

(For the record, I should probably point out, that Maxie is probably right.

Everyone in the entire Known Universe, and Beyond knows the Toxic Spew *is a disgustingly filthy, tatty pile of old junk whose cargo is most likely to be . . . er, a disgustingly filthy, tatty old pile of old junk.*

Even if it is being carted around in a Day-Glo yellow flying saucer.

But on the other hand, and I don't want to alarm you, but there is a chance, just a small chance, she might be wrong.)

Harvey was worried. Very worried. It didn't matter how much the Techno-tium was worth, he'd put the crew at risk, and that was wrong. He kicked himself. Why hadn't he realised that a valuable cargo would make them a target? It was like being the best striker on your team. You were always a magnet for the most, the hardest and the dirtiest tackles.

He sighed. There was no way he could order the crew to leave the Techno-tium now. They'd mutiny.

Pilot Officer Maxie pushed her sleeves up her arms, sat forward at the flight desk and confidently grasped the controls. Using the manifold uplift shunting boosters she nudged the *Toxic Spew* around so the back of the ship faced the giant freight container.

Slow but steady . . .

Then she slowly hauled the flight control joysticks into reverse and the *Toxic Spew* began to move backwards, closing in on the container. As they got closer she activated the rear subatomic tow bar and the reversing bleepers went off.

BEEP . . . BEEP . . . BEEP . . .

Harvey suddenly realised that he couldn't actually see what was happening. The three vast vision screens were at the front and sides of the bridge – but there were none at the back.

Hang on, he thought, *if I can't see what's happening, then how can Maxie?*

(Since you've never reversed a spaceship it might be helpful if I point out that it's quite tricky

because you can't look over your shoulder through
the rear windscreen, or open a window and look
round. So spaceships have all sorts of state-of-the
art reversing kit.

   Well, some of them do.)

'Er, is there a reversing camera, or something?' asked Harvey.

'Yes,' said Gizmo. 'But it's broken.'

'We used to have wing mirrors, but they're broken too,' added Scrummage.

'But how can Maxie see what she's doing?' said Harvey.

'I can't! So shut up! I'm *trying* to listen to the bleeps.'

BEEP . . . BEEP . . . BEEP . . .

'Shhh,' said Gizmo.

'Yes, shhhhh,' added Scrummage, not wanting to be outdone by Gizmo.

The beeps got faster and faster

BEEP – BEEP – BEEP

And then faster still:

BEEP-BEEP-BEEP-BEEP-BEEP-BEEP-BEEP

Until there were one single long

B-B-B-B-B-B-BEEEEEEEEEEEEP!

Harvey held his breath. There was a slight

BUMP

and a soft

CLUNK

as the rear subatomic tow bar of the *Toxic Spew* caught onto the tow hook of the freight container and then Maxie yanked on the supersonic handbrake. Harvey breathed out.

As tough as Yargal's pizza bases

Harvey had seen Maxie fly the *Toxic Spew* in some very tricky situations (actually he'd seen her fly the *Toxic Spew* in some terrifying situations) and knew she was a brilliant pilot. But he was blown away by the fact that she'd just reversed the *Toxic Spew*, with pinpoint accuracy, when she couldn't even see where she was going!

'Pilot Officer Maxie, that was fantastic!' he said.

She turned round and gave him a huge grin. Her bright turquoise eyes shone under her straight multicoloured fringe. 'Thank you, Captain! But that was the easy bit. The hard bit is pulling away.'

Scrummage came over and slapped Harvey on the back. 'Don't worry, Captain. We do this all the time. It's what this little ship is built for! She may look tatty but she's as tough as . . . as one of Yargal's pizza bases!'

Chewing her lip and frowning slightly, Maxie eased the flight control joysticks forward and released the supersonic handbrake. Slowly and surely the *Toxic Spew* moved forward, hauling the massive freight container behind her.

'Well done, Pilot Officer Maxie,' cried Gizmo! 'Yahoo!' cried Scrummage! 'We're rich!'

(I bet you've probably guessed he spoke too soon, haven't you.)

Splattering vomit!

GGRRRRRCHHH

There was a horrible grating noise and the ship juddered worryingly. Maxie froze with her hands on the controls.

The grating noise continued.

GGRRRRRCHHH ...

Gizmo and Harvey leapt to their feet.

'Splattering vomit!' cried Scrummage. 'What's happening?'

'Computer?' said Harvey. 'Give me a damage report.'

'Is that: Give me a damage report, *please?*' snipped the computer.

'No, it's: Give me a damage report *immediately,*' cried Harvey anxiously.

GGRRRRRCHHH . . .

'All right, calm down! No need to get snippy. Well, today's damage report is not encouraging. As well as the usual bumps and scratches and dents, and the general tattiness of the entire ship . . . it appears the rear subatomic tow bar is about to rip off.'

KERRRR-UNCH!!!!

'Correction. The rear subatomic tow bar *has* ripped off!'

It took a nanosecond for this to sink in.

Then the entire crew shared a rare moment of team togetherness and cried:

'NOOOOOOO!'

CHAPTER TEN

Horrible silence and ominous noises

There was a horrible silence on the bridge of the *Toxic Spew*.

It was broken by some truly loud and ominous noises coming from the back of the ship. But without a reversing camera, or any wing mirrors, it was impossible for the crew to see what was happening.

Fortunately, the computer was able to give them a running commentary.

Unfortunately, it was gobthumpingly tactless.

'Oh, whoops!' it said brightly. 'The rear subatomic tow bar has torn clean off its base!'

RIIIIP!

'Oh! And there goes the rubber counter gravity bumper as well.'

GRAAUUNCH!

'And the reactor-driven heat shield.'

KERRRANNNNNG!

'*And* the back booster ramscoop plate! Oh, what a shame, it was all going so well. You must be gutted.' It bleeped off smugly.

Three horrified purple faces turned slowly to look at Harvey.

'Fluttering chunder!' spluttered Scrummage.

'Oh dear,' said Gizmo.

'Well, Captain,' said Maxie. 'What are we going to do now?'

'We're all going to die!'

But before Harvey had time to even think up a plan of action,

SCHWOOOOOOSH!

the doors to the bridge slid open and Yargal wobbled onto the bridge, with Snuffles faithfully following her. Her slug-like body shook violently and her six blue tentacles and yellow eye-stalks flailed about wildly in panic. Flecks of grey snot speckled the deck as she sobbed in fear.

'Captain, CAPTAIN!' she cried, flinging herself at him. 'Save us. Save us! There was a horrible grating noise and the whole ship started juddering and then there was this huge KERRRR-UNCH! And then a RIIIIP! and a GRAAUUNCH! And then a massive KERRRANNNNNG! And I don't like to panic you, but I think *we're all going to die!*'

At this, Snuffles promptly plonked himself down the deck and howled.

AROOOO, AROUOUOU, AROOO, AROUOUOU!

went Snuffles loudly.

WAIL, SOB, SOB SNOT, SOB, SNOT, WAIL!

wept Yargal, even more loudly.

It was chaos. Harvey couldn't hear himself think.

'Quiet, Snuffles, QUIET! Down boy, DOWN!' ordered Harvey, gently patting him on the head, and eventually the huge Hazard Hunting Hound sank to the deck at Harvey's feet whimpering softly.

WHINGE, WHINGE! WHIMPER, WHIMPER!

SupaCool captain

'Calm down, Officer Yargal,' said Harvey reassuringly. He wanted to pat her on the tentacle to sooth her jangling nerves, but she

really was disgustingly slimy. 'We've just lost a few . . . er . . . bits and pieces off the back of the ship. Nothing to worry about.'

The crew were well impressed. No, make that gobstoppered. In all their multiple intergalactic missions they had never seen a captain take so much disaster so calmly.

At this point the back booster ramscoop plate and the rubber counter gravity bumper drifted across the front vision screen. But Harvey just ignored them.

From the flight desk, Maxie grinned at Harvey. 'That's the spirit, Captain,' she said. 'So again, what are we going to do?'

'If I were Captain . . .' said Gizmo.

'Well, you're not,' interrupted Scrummage. 'And since I'm the Chief Rubbish Officer, it's my decision. I say we just transport onto the cargo container, grab the Techno-tium, come back and leave the container to drift harmlessly in space.'

'Sounds good to me,' said Maxie.

But Gizmo was outraged. 'We're not pirates!' he spluttered. 'And since you're the chief Bin Man . . .'

'Chief *Rubbish Officer*!' snapped Scrummage.

Gizmo ignored him and carried on sternly. 'Then I shouldn't have to remind you of the Intergalactic Travel and Transport Pact rules and regulations regarding rubbish retrieval. Captain, what Scrummage is suggesting is highly irregular, irresponsible and downright illegal.'

(To be fair to Gizmo, I should point out that he's absolutely right.

Nothing the size of a SupaCosmicCargo Company container can just 'drift harmlessly' in space.

It's far more likely to 'drift' onto a SuperSpaceWay in the rush hour or into a pangalactic tourist cruiser carrying hundreds of beings to popular holiday planets all over Galaxy 43b.

Ouch, that would be messy.)

'Oh, Captain,' cried Yargal, her tentacles writhing anxiously. 'What are we going to do?'

'Yes, Captain,' said Maxie, her bright turquoise eyes challenging him from beneath her long straight fringe, and her elbows on the flight desk. 'Yet again, what are we going to do?'

CHAPTER ELEVEN

Team spirit

In all honesty Harvey didn't know what to do. But he *did* know that the crew would turn into a bunch of bickering intergalactic bin men if he let them know that. You can't let a crew lose confidence in the captain. It's bad for team spirit.

So he said in a confident tone, 'Officer Gizmo is right. We're responsible for that cargo container and . . .'

'Um, technically *we're* not,' cut in Gizmo. '*You are*. You're the captain.'

'And *you* signed the digiforms,' said

Scrummage.

'Yup, you're on your own on this one,' said Maxie.

Thanks a bunch, thought Harvey, *so much for team spirit*.

'Computer, do you have any suggestions?' he asked.

'Of course I do,' snapped the computer, bleeping importantly. 'But first can I just check how much space travel insurance you have?'

'Er . . . none,' said Harvey.

Gizmo gasped softly and Scrummage whistled in his teeth.

'Blimey, you're braver than you look,' said Maxie.

'Yes,' said the computer, its lights flickering on and off smugly. 'I wouldn't want to be in your space boots if the Intergalactic Traffic Police find out!

'Well, in that case, given:

a) the size of the container and
b) the damage and deaths it could cause,
c) the fact that you *personally* signed for it and
d) that you have no space travel insurance
   and last but not least
e) the danger of a murderous bunch of space pirates pitching up and slitting your gizzards . . .

then I suggest we do a runner.'

Team panic

Maxie swung round back to the flight desk. 'Right, let's get out of here. Standing by for cosmic speed, Captain,' she said, frantically punching buttons and taking the supersonic handbrake off.

'Nooooo!' cried Scrummage, desperate at losing the Techno-tium.

'Yes!' cried Yargal, who didn't fancy hanging around and waiting for a bunch of space pirates to do the gizzard-splitting thing.

'No!' cried Gizmo, who didn't want to abandon the cargo container.

'Again, standing by for cosmic speed, Captain,' reminded Maxie urgently.

There was a tiny nanobeat before Harvey spoke and four faces and nine eyes turned to stare at him in disbelief.

'Stand down Maxie,' he said calmly.

You didn't get chosen to captain the Highford All Stars for two years if you gave up and ran away when things got tough. Harvey had been picked, not just because he was talented, but because he knew all the other players' skills. He knew their strengths and their weaknesses. And *he never let them give up.*

So he stood his ground, and chose his words carefully.

Team talk

'We're not going to abandon the cargo container and run away.' Turning to Gizmo he said, 'One, putting others at risk is irresponsible.'

And then he looked at Yargal. 'Two, running away to save ourselves and leaving others in danger is cowardly.'

'Three, running away before there's anything to run away from is pointless,' he said to Maxie.

Finally, looking at Scrummage he said: 'And four, leaving the Techno-tium for another team . . . er, space crew to grab is stupid.

'We can do this. And in fact *we have* to do this – because we're the crew of the *Toxic Spew*, and we're the only bin men in Galaxy 43b. So the only question is how?'

CHAPTER TWELVE

A big problem

If you'd slapped the crew round the face with a wet muddy football sock, they couldn't have been more surprised. They looked at Harvey with great respect. He might only be eleven, and from a planet no one had ever heard of, but in all their multiple intergalactic missions, Harvey was turning out to be the best captain the *Toxic Spew* had ever had.

Gizmo spoke for them all when he said quietly, 'Well said, sir.'

So the crew sat and pondered how to fix the cargo container to the *Toxic Spew*. It was a big problem – but then it was a big container.

(It might surprise you to learn that although the Toxic Spew is the tattiest, grubbiest and least space-worthy ship in the whole of Galaxy 43b it does have some really snazzy, top-of-the-range, rubbish collection equipment.

And it will definitely surprise you to learn that Scrummage actually knows how to use it.

It certainly surprises me.)

Some rubbish suggestions

'Could we use the magnet beam thingy?' asked Harvey.

Scrummage raised one white eyebrow and looked at him witheringly. 'Do you mean the Zenith Mark 4 Magno Beam?'

Stuck on the front of the ship, this enormous magnet can pull massive chunks of junk metal towards the *Toxic Spew*.

'Negative,' said Gizmo. 'The cargo container's

made of carbi-fibre, so it's not magnetic.'

'How about the rubbish net?' said Maxie, winding Scrummage up.

Scrummage flinched. 'Do you mean the Nebula 30X-1 multi-stranded meteorite-proof mesh mechanism?'

'Yeah, the rubbish net,' said Maxie, grinning at Harvey, who tried to keep a straight face.

Scrummage shook his head. 'The container's way too big.' He leant over the garbage controls desk, drumming his grubby fingers on the grimy surface. 'That only leaves the Ultrawave 3.2 Vac Tube . . .'

'What, the sucky-up thing?' said Maxie mischievously.

'The sucky-up thing!' spluttered Scrummage.

(Scrummage was enormously proud of the Toxic Spew's *Ultrawave 3.2 Vac Tube.*

To be fair, it is a pretty classy piece of kit. It's made of 100% pure bonded Stainless Bond-ite and has three hose attachments: Nova Nozzle, Super Nova Nozzle and Super Nova Nozzle Plus.

And it's gobsplutteringly powerful.

You probably can't even begin to imagine how strong it is. The vacuum cleaners on your planet are puny little machines that can only pick up tiny things like biscuit crumbs, dog hairs, and small plastic toy building bricks.

I mean be honest, there's no way they could pick up, say, a child-sized bike or a fridge freezer, is there? Let alone an enormous freight container.)

'Don't be ridiculous!' cried Yargal. 'You can't vacuum up the container, it's enormous! It won't go up the nozzle!'

'Candy-coloured upchuck!' said Scrummage. 'That's it!'

Supernova nozzle plus

Feverishly he flicked switches, punched buttons and hauled levers on the garbage control desk. 'I'll put it onto Super Nova Nozzle Plus suction power . . .'

'Ooooh,' said Maxie, 'super suck!'

Scrummage ignored her. 'The container will get sucked, er, I mean *vacuumed* onto the end of the nozzle and if I keep the suction power on FULL we can tow it to an interstellar scrapyard on the end of the hose.'

Harvey slapped Scrummage on the back. 'Brilliant! Well done, Rubbish Officer Scrummage.'

'Thank you, sir,' said Scrummage, trying to look modest.

Maxie looked for the nearest interstellar scrapyard on the 3D digital star map. It was Quasar Quick Fix and Quality Parts, about 3.4 zillion cosmic kilometres away on the other side of the Green Gallipian roundabout.

Harvey ordered the computer to plot the best route. He said 'best' rather than 'quickest' because the computer would blissfully send them hurtling into certain death traps like meteorite belts, toxic gas clouds and molten lava pools just to save a few seconds.

Harvey got Maxie to check the computer's sums, and then they plotted the route again.

It was going to take several hours to get to the scrapyard, and since it was already late, Harvey ordered everyone to go their quarters to get some rest. Yargal headed off saying she'd bring them all some pizza for supper.

'And please, can I just have cheese and tomato? With absolutely no rocket fuel sauce!' Harvey called after her.

'Wimp!' laughed Maxie.

CHAPTER THIRTEEN

Captain's quarters

The captain's quarters of the *Toxic Spew* are a bit basic. There's a metal bunk screwed to the floor with roll-out drawers underneath, and a large monitor with SpaceTime connection mounted on the wall. And, er . . . that's it.

When Harvey had first seen his quarters, they were utterly trashed. The bedclothes were thrown in a tangled heap on the floor, and the whole room was strewn with empty drinks cartons, chocolate bar wrappers, empty crisp packets, dirty underwear, and a very smelly old pair of space boots. But Yargal had kindly

helped him clean it out a bit. And now it was astonishingly tidy.

It's amazing how much you can do in thirty seconds when you have six tentacles and a large bin liner.

It's also amazing how tidy you can keep things if you don't have any things. (Technically of course, Harvey has plenty of stuff – but it's all in his bedroom, which is several gazillion light years away on the other side of the universe.)

Captain's kit

Harvey had arrived on the *Toxic Spew* in his school uniform and with absolutely nothing else. But the crew had managed to get the bare essentials for him:

a uniform (several sizes too large)
a toothbrush
toothpaste
spare underpants and socks
a games console with a stack of games

a hot chocolate machine

a handheld 3V VidiScreen with full Outernet connection

a jelly bean dispenser

two build your own model spaceships with moving parts, and

some tatty old dog-eared spaceship manuals.

Harvey put a plastic cup in the hot chocolate machine and pressed the button. It was great having it in his quarters, but he missed his mum's hot chocolate. She did it with a swirl of squirty cream sprinkled with mini marshmallows and topped off with crumbly chocolate. The stuff from the machine wasn't nearly as good.

Then he curled up on the bunk. Snuffles leapt up, dug around at the duvet for a bit, until he'd pulled most of it off Harvey and under his huge shaggy belly, and then plonked himself heavily down against Harvey's legs.

Harvey could have sent Snuffles to sleep in his basket, but he liked the hound – even if it was difficult to sleep with him taking up so much more than his fair share of the bed, and snoring more loudly than a subsonic booster engine with a dodgy silencer.

As Harvey zzz'd off, the *Toxic Spew* slipped silently through the utter blackness of deep space – a brave little ship dwarfed by the absolute and incredible enormity of the universe all around her.

Very, very long lists

At the engineering desk, Gizmo drew up a list of spare parts needed to repair, or replace the broken bits on the ship. With a bit of luck they could pick some up from the interstellar scrapyard. It was a very, very long list.

(If you don't like lists, or you're not mechanically minded, you can skip this bit. Since you're from Earth, none of it will mean very much to you anyway.

But if you are interested in spaceship design
you might like to know his list included:
    rear subatomic tow bar
    rubber counter gravity bumper
    reactor-driven heat shield
    back booster ramscoop plate
    reversing camera and
    2 wing mirrors.
    And that was just the stuff needed on the outside
of the ship.)

Scrummage sat with his grimy space boots up on the garbage control desk, his grubby hands folded on his huge belly, keeping his eye on the controls of the Ultrawave 3.2 Vac Tube. He drew up a mental list of all the things he could buy once they'd flogged the Techno-tium. It was a very, very long list. Much longer than Gizmo's.

(You probably really don't want to read another
list here, do you? So maybe I'll just say it started
modestly enough with a personal pizza dispenser

and unlimited supplies of mozzarella, chocolate,
banana custard and chilli sauce.

Then it got rather more ambitious, by which I
mean, downright greedy, until it ended with:

a small planet with sandy white beaches and
a heated sea.)

An ominously large ship

While the *Toxic Spew* zoomed along, with a
cargo of the most valuable metal in the entire
Known Universe, and Beyond, an ominously
large spaceship loomed out the blackness of
deep space. It seemed to be following them.

Scrummage and Gizmo didn't notice. Partly
because they were busy making lists, but mostly
because the *Toxic Spew* didn't have a reversing
camera or any wing mirrors.

And the computer didn't mention it either.

(This might have been because the computer was
sulking. It had been in a snippy mood all day.

Or it might have been because it didn't think the ominously large ship was anything to worry about.

Or it might have been because it was so busy playing itself at MeteoriteMaze 3 that it just hadn't noticed.

Look, I don't want to make a huge dramatic moment here. It might be perfectly innocent.

On the other hand, it might not.)

CHAPTER FOURTEEN

Harvey oversleeps

BLEEP!

BLEEP!

BLEEP!

A few hours later, Harvey was woken by an urgent bleeping. It was Maxie at the flight control desk, trying to raise him on intership SpaceTime.

Sleepily Harvey shoved Snuffles off his legs and then scrambled over the giant hound to the monitor in the wall and clicked Connect.

'Sorry to wake you, Captain, but I thought you might like to know we'll be at Quasar Quick Fix and Quality Parts in a few minutes.' And before Harvey could reply, or even smarm down his unruly mop of curly hair, she bleeped off.

'Gizmo, you were meant to wake me!' said Harvey crossly as he strode onto the command bridge.

'There was no need, sir, I was quite competently in command,' replied Gizmo casually, still sitting in the captain's chair.

'Thank you,' said Harvey dryly, 'but I'll take command now.'

'Are you sure, sir? I mean, have you had any breakfast yet?' said Gizmo, making no effort to get up.

Harvey gave him a pointed stare and Gizmo reluctantly left his seat. 'Officer Scrummage, give me a status report, please,' said Harvey.

Scrummage yawned, scratched his huge belly

and assured Harvey the container cargo was still safely attached to the nozzle of the Ultrawave 3.2 Vac Tube.

A few moments later Yargal brought Harvey a banana and chocolate breakfast pizza. Which should have been great. But she hadn't been able to resist adding some tuna and chilli cheese melt to jazz it up. Oh, yuk.

Could have been worse, thought Harvey, taking a bite. *At least there's no rocket fuel sauce.*

The big scrapyard in the sky

Tucked away in a quiet corner of Galaxy 43b, Quasar Quick Fix and Quality Parts is one of the biggest spaceship scrapyards in outer space. Hundreds of broken down and abandoned spacecraft of all different types just hang there. From a distance it looks like a small asteroid belt. But as you get closer you can see the shapes of the various spacecraft. And as you get closer still you see the state of them – tatty and decrepit.

(Not as tatty and decrepit as the Toxic Spew *of course. You know, the more I think about it the more I realise how brave the crew are just to go in it.*

It's a miracle it's still flying, it really is.)

As the little garbage ship neared the yard, Maxie cut the engines back and expertly slid the ship into orbital drive and they slowly circled the scrapyard, looking for the best route in between the ships.

Harvey was stunned that so many spaceships had all just been abandoned.

'Where have they all come from?'

'Everyone chucks away their old spaceships when they upgrade to a new one,' said Scrummage.

'Doesn't anyone want them?'

'Nobody would be seen dead in a tatty old

out-of-date spaceship,' said Maxie.

'Apart from us,' said Gizmo gloomily.

'But it's so wasteful!' cried Harvey.

'What do you do with your old spaceships in your galaxy then?' asked Maxie.

Harvey suddenly realised he had no idea.

(As a matter of fact, for a planet that hardly does any space travel, your little planet has chucked huge quantities of space scrap into its orbit. You have no idea how much cosmic garbage there is floating about 250 miles above your head. There's about half a million bits of it, from flakes of paint to entire satellites.

And just because you can't see it, doesn't mean that you shouldn't do something about it. It's like shoving everything under your bed and saying you've tidied your room. It's a disgrace.

I dread to think what your skies will be like if you ever launch a serious programme of space travel.

So there's no need for you to feel smug, is there?)

Harvey didn't get a chance to answer Maxie's excellent question because just at that moment the computer blipped into life. It had finally noticed the ominously large spaceship that seemed to be following them.

The ominously large spaceship, again

'I hate to interrupt you, Captain, because I'm sure you're terribly busy doing something desperately important like eating your breakfast. But I thought I ought to let you know there's an ominously large ship that seems to be following us.'

'What?' cried Harvey and the entire crew in one voice.

'What sort of ship?' said Maxie.

'An ominously large one,' said the computer.

'No, stupid,' said Maxie impatiently, 'I mean is it friendly, or . . . or . . . is it a pirate ship?'

'How would I know? Why don't you ask it! And may I remind you I have a 215 megatronbyte boogleplex memory, so don't call me "stupid", stupid!' snipped the computer, bleeping off.

'Computer, contact the ship and ask them to identify themselves,' ordered Harvey. The computer didn't respond. It was sulking. 'Please!' added Harvey. There was still no reply.

'I'll do it, Captain,' said Gizmo. And he busily flicked switches on his engineering desk. Then he flicked them again, but more urgently. 'They're not responding,' he said.

'Try again,' said Harvey. Gizmo did so, but there was still no reply.

(Again, I don't want to alarm you. The ship-to-ship SpaceTime system on the Toxic Spew *isn't exactly in good nick, and sometimes it works so badly it would be better to just shout. Except that of course sound doesn't travel through space. So it might just be that the other ship simply didn't get the signal, and there's nothing to worry about.*

On the other hand, the brave but mucky crew of the Toxic Spew *might be being chased by some*

of the most vicious and ferocious space pirates
in the entire Known Universe, and Beyond.
  Who knows?)

CHAPTER FIFTEEN

Spaceship graveyard

'Splattering puke! I don't like this, Captain,' said Scrummage anxiously from the garbage control desk.

Harvey didn't like it either. Warning bells were screaming in his head, but he didn't want to alarm the crew so he said calmly: 'We'll soon tell if they're following us. Maxie, head into the scrap yard and see if it follows us.'

'Aye, aye, sir.'

Through the vast vision screens Harvey watched as they drew closer to the giant cluster of spaceships in the scrap yard. Scrummage was still carefully towing the cargo container attached to the nozzle of the Ultrawave 3.2 Vac Tube.

Flying past dozens of abandoned spaceships that were just silently hanging in space, with absolutely no signs of life was frankly spooky. It was like a graveyard of deserted ships – and a haunted one at that.

The gaps between the spaceships seemed worryingly small to Harvey. But, as usual, he was blown away by Maxie's piloting skills as she skilfully swooped and swerved round the abandoned craft looking for the office.

And, to everyone's relief, the ominously large ship that had seemed to be following them *didn't* follow them into the scrapyard.

(See, I told you it might be nothing to worry about.)

Quasar Quick Fix and Quality Parts

The office of Quasar Quick Fix and Quality

Parts Depot is a small, shabby space station Portakabin surrounded by several docking bays. Clear plasti-glass space-gangways connect the bays to the office. It looks like a cross between a snow dome, a marble run and a giant spider.

> *(Look, I realise that's probably not a very helpful description, but is it my fault that you have so little experience of interplanetary exploration on your planet?*
>
> *I mean, if you'd taken the trouble to get out and about a bit in outer space you would have seen an interstellar scrapyard and I wouldn't have to try to describe one to you, would I?*
>
> *So don't blame me.)*

Maxie skilfully docked the *Toxic Spew* in an empty bay with the exit pod perfectly lined up to the airlock entry, and hauled on the supersonic handbrake. The cargo container took up another four parking spaces behind them.

Scrummage turned the Ultrawave 3.2 Vac Tube down to Nova Power. 'Shall we go,

Captain?' he said, heading off the bridge.

'Er, yes,' said Harvey, following him and wondering how they were actually going to get from the *Toxic Spew* to the scrapyard office. He'd had one terrifying experience of being stranded outside in the utter airlessness of space and didn't fancy another one. But he didn't want to show his ignorance and decided to trust his Rubbish Officer to get him there safely.

'Assuming command, sir,' said Gizmo crisply and headed for the captain's chair. Maxie groaned dramatically and rolled her turquoise eyes under her multicoloured fringe.

Gizmo ignored her and handed Harvey his digipad with the list of spare parts. 'I doubt we'll be able to get them all, sir,' he said. 'But I've put the most vital ones at the top.'

Don't panic!

Harvey followed Scrummage along the dank, dimly lit and frankly filthy corridors to the exit pod of the *Toxic Spew*. You'd expect to hear their feet clanging on the metal floors. But all you could hear was a disgustingly sticky slurp as their feet peeled off the tacky surface. The stench of rotting rubbish that clung throughout the ship made Harvey's eyes water. He clenched his teeth and tried not to gag.

After a few gobsmackingly gross minutes, they arrived at the exit pod.

(Again, since you're from Earth you probably haven't been on a single spaceship, have you? So you don't have a clue what the exit pod looks like. Even though it's a perfectly normal one.

Imagine a short, round corridor with a circular door at each end. Then imagine it covered in piles of tatty old spacesuits, boots and helmets just strewn all over the floor.

And finally, imagine the walls, floor and doors smeared with thick dollops of muck and grime. You know, the kind you have to scrape off with a blunt knife or your fingernail.)

SCHWOOOSH!

The door slid open and they went in. Harvey bent down to pick up a spacesuit, but to his amazement, Scrummage calmly stepped over the pile of space kit and start to open the *outside* door.

'Er, haven't you forgotten something?' said Harvey pointedly.

'Oh, sorry,' said Scrummage, stepping aside. 'After you, Captain.'

That's not what I meant, thought Harvey. His heart pounded with fear as he stood, without so much as a pair of swimming goggles for protection, at the exit hatch of the *Toxic Spew*. It began to slide open.

Don't panic, he told himself. *Scrummage might be reckless, but he's not that stupid. If he needed a spacesuit he would have remembered to put one on. So calm down, you are not going to die,* he told himself. But his brain disagreed and screamed silently in his head.

AAAAAAARGH!

CHAPTER SIXTEEN

Another human!?

SCHWHOOOOSH!

The exit hatch hissed open to an air-conditioned tunnel, with see-through sides, that had automatically sealed itself onto the outside of the *Toxic Spew*. A strip of lights ran along the floor, guiding the way to the office. *This is AWESOME,* thought Harvey as they trudged along the walkway, with millions of stars and a handful of planets all around him, beyond the clear plasti-glass walls.

As they got near the office, Scrummage turned to Harvey and patted the side of his nose.

'Leave it to me to do the talking,' he said. 'The scrap merchant's a bit of a rogue but we're old mates and he'll do me a good deal.'

Fine by me, thought Harvey. Then he realised he was just about to meet another alien and didn't want to offend anyone by overreacting (or even fainting) so he asked Scrummage what sort of alien to expect.

'Alien? He isn't an alien!' said Scrummage.

A human? thought Harvey. *Another human!* And then another brilliant, massive and incredible thought struck him: *he'll know how to get back to Earth!* Harvey was ecstatic and a huge grin spread across his face. He couldn't wait to meet him.

The plasti-glass walkway ended in a dull grey wall with a door to one side. The words 'Quasar Quick Fix and Quality Parts – OFFICE' were scrawled messily on the door in what looked to Harvey, suspiciously like felt-tip pen. As soon as they approached, the door slid open automatically with a horrible grating noise that set Harvey's teeth on edge.

Well, to be honest, it slid open partly and then stuck. Harvey could just about slip through but Scrummage had to force it open with his shoulder to squeeze his plump (actually, make that fat) body into the office.

The scrap merchant was leaning behind a high counter in the middle of the office. Behind him a tatty poster of lots of different spaceships was tacked onto the grubby wall. Taller than Gizmo and wider than Scrummage, he was as big as a bear. And he had a purple face, turquoise eyes and multicoloured hair. He was obviously from Zeryx Minor.

Harvey was gutted.

(If you've got a bit confused here it might help if I explain how the whole 'alien' thing works throughout the entire Known Universe, and Beyond.

118

It's quite simple.

Someone from your own planet is not an alien – even if you meet them on another planet. But if you meet someone from another planet then they <u>are</u> an alien. Unless you're on their planet, in which case you're an alien and they're not.

And if two aliens from different planets meet a third alien on his or her or its world, then the first two aliens are both aliens and the third alien isn't. But if they all met up on a fourth planet then they're all aliens. Are you keeping up?

And if two aliens from the same world meet a third alien on his or her or its world, then the first two aliens are not aliens to each other but they are aliens to the third alien, who is not an alien. See? Simple.)

Scrummage does the talking

'Takki, you old rascal!' cried Scrummage.

'Scrummage, you old scoundrel!' beamed the scrap merchant leaning over the counter to give

Scrummage a hearty wallop on the back. They laughed and thumped each other happily for a short while and then Scrummage introduced Harvey.

'Blimey, he's a bit young for a captain, isn't he?' said Takki.

'Yes but he's *brilliant*,' bragged Scrummage, putting his arm around Harvey proudly. 'He made captain aged nine.'

Harvey winced inwardly but managed a weak smile. *I really am going to have to tell them that the Highford All Stars is a football team,* he thought.

'A captain at nine?! Blimey, young man!' said Takki and shot a respectful look at Harvey. 'You're a bit smart then. Tell you what, why don't you leave Scrummage to do the talking!' And his purple face broke into a huge grin.

Harvey grinned back. The scrap merchant looked well dodgy, but he instantly liked him. You knew where you were with people like him. They'd rob you blind if you gave them a chance, and they didn't pretend otherwise.

'So what brings you to this distant corner of Galaxy 43b?' asked Takki.

Scrummage rubbed his hands together eagerly. 'We've got a bit a business to put your way. We've got a SupaCosmicCargo container in excellent condition. We'll swap it for these.' And he handed Takki Gizmo's digipad with the long list of parts the *Toxic Spew* needed.

> *(I don't know if you need a reminder, but here's the list of Gizmo's 'must haves':*
> > *rear subatomic tow bar*
> > *rubber counter gravity bumper*
> > *reactor-driven heat shield*
> > *back booster ramscoop plate*
> > *reversing camera and*
> > *2 wing mirrors)*

Takki scanned the list then roared with laughter. 'Good grief! Is that ship actually space-worthy? In fact, is it even safe?'

Scrummage grinned. 'Probably not!'

Takki turned to Harvey. 'Blimey,' he joked,

'you've got to be brave to fly in that!'

'Yup,' said Harvey. 'The crew of the *Toxic Spew* are a pretty brave bunch.'

Scrummage hitched up his overalls and tried to look modest.

Takki does the talking

'Tell you what,' said Takki, 'I get the container *and* the cargo and you get a rear subatomic tow bar, a back booster ramscoop plate and two wing mirrors. Can't say fairer than that!'

'No chance!' exclaimed Scrummage hotly. 'We get the cargo! There's absolutely no way we're giving away the cargo.'

Takki leant forward on his counter with interest. 'Oh yeah? Why, what's in there then?'

'Er . . . I don't know,' lied Scrummage, badly, and trying to shrug casually.

Takki's turquoise eyes narrowed with suspicion under his white eyebrows. 'Why don't you know? Is it stolen?'

'Mottled vomit!' cried Scrummage. 'Would I do that to you?'

'Yes,' said Takki simply. 'So, again, why don't you know what's in the container?'

'Er . . . er . . .' stammered Scrummage.

Harvey does the talking

Harvey spoke up. He wasn't going to lie to Takki. But he wasn't going to give him the whole story either.

'We answered a distress signal from the SupaCosmicCargo Delivery Company. The couriers said they weren't responsible for the quantity, colour or existence of the cargo,' he said, with total honesty. 'Or feeding, watering or exercising it,' he added.

There was a beat and then Takki rocked backwards with laughter. 'Are you mad? There could be anything in there from a pile of worthless space junk, to crates of deadly poisonous toxic gas or a writhing heap of Giant

Space Slop Worms that'll suck you to death! Well, in that case, I'll take the container and you can definitely keep the cargo.'

'But what about the spare parts?' asked Harvey, tapping the digipad.

'I said you were a smart one,' said Takki. There was a sharp intake of breath as he scanned the list again. 'OK, I can let you have a back booster ramscoop plate and two wing mirrors.'

'Can't you sling in a rear subatomic tow bar, just for old time's sake?' pleaded Scrummage.

'Oh, go on then. But you're robbing me blind.' And he shook hands, first with Scrummage and then with Harvey and the deal was done.

Red alert!

As soon they got back to the command bridge Harvey ordered the computer to transport the cargo straight into the hold of the *Toxic Spew*.

Then Maxie expertly slid the ship's controls out of orbital drive and took off the supersonic handbrake.

She pushed her sleeves up her arms, sat forward at the flight desk and using the manifold shunting boosters she slowly pulled away from the docking bay of the Quasar Quick Fix and Quality Parts interstellar scrapyard and into hyperspace.

As soon as the *Toxic Spew* was safely clear, Harvey and Scrummage literally ran down to the cargo bay, desperate to see how much Techno-tium there was.

And just how rich – how *very, very rich* they all were.

But they'd only just got to the cargo hold doors when suddenly:

RED ALERT! RED ALERT!

WHOOP! WHOOP! WHOOP!

'Captain to the bridge, Captain to the bridge!' screamed the computer hysterically:

'WE'RE UNDER ATTACK!'

CHAPTER SEVENTEEN

Under attack

ZAP! ZAP! ZAP!

Harvey and Scrummage raced back onto the bridge.

ZAP! ZAP! ZAP!

RED ALERT! RED ALERT!

WHOOP! WHOOP! WHOOP!

'Fluttering vomit!' cried Scrummage.

'Shields up!' yelled Harvey to Maxie.

'Oh, I wish I'd thought of that,' she yelled sarcastically from the flight desk. 'On no, wait, I did. Otherwise we'd have been crushed to a pulp, pulverised to a paste, pounded to a powder, and scattered to the ends of the entire Known Universe, and Beyond!'

Harvey took this in for a nanosecond and said. 'Thank you, well done, Officer Maxie.'

ZAP! ZAP-A-ZAP! ZAP!

Streaks of blazing red rays blasted against the ship's shields and lit the bridge with hot streaked lightning. The *Toxic Spew* juddered and trembled (and so did the crew) and it was all Maxie could do to keep the ship level. It was like being in a violent indoor thunderstorm (but without the rain).

SCHWOOOSH!

Suddenly the doors to the bridge slid opened.

Not now, Yargal!

'Lunchtime!' cried Yargal gaily and she slurped onto the bridge, her tentacles full of pizza boxes and drinks cartons.

Snuffles plodded closely behind her, drooling hopefully. Long strings of saliva dripped off his huge teeth.

'And, Captain, I made you a plain cheese and tomato one without even the teeny tiniest smidgeon of rocket fuel sauce!' said Yargal with pride.

'Not now!' cried Harvey. 'We're under attack!'

ZAP! ZAP-A-ZAP-A-ZAP! ZAP!

RED ALERT! RED ALERT!

WHOOP! WHOOP! WHOOP!

'Aaaaaargh!' screamed Yargal. 'We're under attack!'

Her blue tentacles flailed violently and the

pizza boxes crashed to the floor and burst open. Snuffles was on them in a flash and wolfing down pizza as if it was the last meal he was ever going to get. Which, given the crisis on the bridge, was very possible.

Oh, yuk!

Yargal was terrified. Her body oozed thick yellow sweat and strings of slimy grey snot splattered everywhere as she sobbed and hiccupped violently.

She was without doubt the most disgusting thing Harvey had ever seen. He froze, staring at her in utter revulsion. Then she flung herself into his arms.

SPLAT!

(That's the one snag of having a Yargillian on the bridge at a time of crisis. They're very soggy when they panic and they don't keep it to themselves.)

'Save me,' she cried!

Oh yuk, thought Harvey, as strands of snot flickered onto his face and trails of gunk slimed his school uniform. But to his enormous credit, he kept both his nerve and his manners. Calmly and gently he pushed her towards the Chief Rubbish Officer, who was the least busy member of the bridge crew at that moment.

'Scrummage, look after Yargal.'

ZAP-A-ZAP-A-ZAP!

RED ALERT! RED ALERT!

WHOOP! WHOOP! WHOOP!

'What are we going to do?' yelled Maxie, wrestling with the flight controls and desperately trying to keep the ship steady.

'The shields aren't going to stand much more of this, Captain,' warned Gizmo, frantically punching buttons at the engineering desk.

The ominously large spaceship, yet again.

'Computer, give me a damage report,' ordered Harvey.

BLEEP, BLIBBLE, BLEEP!

went the computer, then it said casually, 'Well, I could do, but in all honesty, is it worth it? You're all going to die anyway. I may as well go back to my game.' And it bleeped off.

Before the crew could take in this dire, if not totally unexpected news, the ominously large ship that had seemed to be following them, suddenly zipped into view on the front vision screen.

Menacing, shiny and jet-black, it glittered and gleamed with glitzy space bling. The sleek lines of the ship were picked out in large flashy fake diamonds. And its front bumper was edged with yellow and green gems mounted in gold trim.

It was glossy and glassy.

But it certainly wasn't classy.

There was a nanosecond of a pause and then three Zeryx Minors and one Yargillion all went:

'AAAAAAAARGH!'

'BLING BOTS!'

CHAPTER EIGHTEEN

Terror on the command bridge

SCRABBLE THUMP!

Scrummage flung himself under the garbage control desk.

SCRABBLE, SCRABBLE!

'Move over!'

THUMP!

Maxie joined him and:

BLEURGH!

Gizmo vomited in pure terror into a plastic cup and then crumpled into a collapsed heap in his seat.

WHIMPER, WHINE!

Snuffles flattened his huge body down onto the deck and put his massive fluffy paws over his eyes. His meatball of a nose quivered and cringed. And,

SLAP, SPLAT!

Yargal fainted and hit the deck, hard.

Captain Harvey Drew, the eleven-year-old commander of the *Toxic Spew* was the only man left standing.

> *(I'm sorry to interrupt the story at this electrifying moment, but you have absolutely no idea why the crew are so petrified, and I wouldn't want*

you to think it's because they're cowards.

The Bling Bots from the planet Sy-Boorg in the Droid Galaxy are the most notorious and ruthless pirates in the entire Known Universe, and Beyond.

To give you some idea of just how bad they are, they're worse than the vicious Vultons from the Carrion Cluster in Galaxy 6, and even worse than the TerrorDactoids from the Terbium Matrix Belt and far, far worse than . . .

Actually, you've never heard of any of these aliens, have you? So none of this means anything to you, does it?

You really do lead a sheltered life on your little planet, don't you?

Lucky you.)

Ship-to-ship SpaceTime

To Harvey's surprise, the Bling Bots suddenly stopped firing. A small icon appeared on the monitor at Gizmo's engineering control desk asking for ship-to-ship SpaceTime.

'They want to make contact,' whimpered Gizmo anxiously.

But:

RED ALERT! RED ALERT!

WHOOP! WHOOP! WHOOP!

The ships alarms were still screaming so loudly that Harvey could hardly hear Gizmo, and worse, he could hardly hear himself think. And just right now, he needed a really clear head.

'Computer, cut alarms,' he ordered.

'Oh, are you still alive? What a lovely surprise!' said the computer brightly. 'Of course, you might live to regret it. The Bling Bots are very keen on inflicting terribly slow and dreadfully painful deaths. But anyhow, cutting alarms.'

The sudden silence on the bridge was nerve wracking. All Harvey could hear was the **BLEEP! BLEEP!** alert of the ship-to-ship SpaceTime request.

Yargal was still out cold on the deck. A pool of grey slime gathered around her. Maxie and Scrummage were cowering under their desks while Gizmo sat trembling violently. He had gone a very pale purple. Snuffles had gone very quiet. He was playing dead. Smart dog.

Another team pep talk

Harvey took a deep breath. He might not be the most experienced spaceship captain in the entire Known Universe, and Beyond, but he had plenty of experience of captaining the weaker team. The Highford All Stars were nowhere near the top of the league and had to face really tough opponents almost every Sunday. And it wasn't just the team. The mums and dads could be horrendous.

But you couldn't let that intimidate you. He'd known teams lose a match before they'd even left the changing rooms. The captain's job is to make his team believe they can win. It was time for a team pep talk.

'Right . . . er . . . Bin Men,' he said. 'Listen up. I haven't been Captain of the *Toxic Spew* for very long, but in that time you've really impressed me by getting through some deadly dangerous situations.

'You've faced poisonous killer maggots, a multiple spacecraft pile-up on the HyperspaceWay, and lethal exploding garbage that sent us spiralling off completely out of control.

'And I bet that before I joined you, you probably faced all sort of lots of other dire and dreadful challenges . . . and you obviously coped with them all or you wouldn't be here now.

'So, Officers Scrummage and Maxie, please return to your stations. Officer Gizmo, standby to accept the ship-to-ship SpaceTime connection. Snuffles, sit . . . SIT! Good dog. And, Yargal . . . Yargal?'

But Yargal was still out cold – which was probably a good thing.

Bring it on

Sheepishly, Scrummage and Maxie clambered back into their seats, Scrummage only pausing to bravely hitch up his overalls. Maxie pushed up her sleeves and Gizmo sat bolt upright in his seat. Snuffles sat with his back against Harvey's legs. To be fair to them, in all their multiple intergalactic missions, the Bin Men of the *Toxic Spew* had never, ever had to face anything so utterly and completely terrifying as Bling Bots. And it was frankly staggering that Harvey had managed to rally his team . . . er, crew, at all.

'Are we ready on the bridge?' he asked calmly.

'Yes, sir,' replied the crew.

Harvey flicked his fringe off his forehead and leant forward on the arm of the chair in what he hoped looked like a firm and commanding position. 'Right then, Officer Gizmo, let's meet the opposition.'

CHAPTER NINETEEN

Bling Bots!

Trying to control his trembling fingers, Officer Gizmo clicked to accept the ship-to-ship SpaceTime connection. An image appeared on the front vision screen – it took up almost the entire screen.

A hideously ugly alien stared silently, and threateningly at Harvey.

Harvey flinched inwardly but forced himself not to react. But Snuffles shot to his feet with his hackles up. He bared his teeth and snarled furiously. Dribbles of drool dripped onto the deck.

DROOL! DRIBBLE! DROOL!

(If you have a weak stomach, or if you've just eaten, you might want to give this next bit a miss.)

Bling Bots are half robot and half space worm. They look like metal beetles with a sweaty, bare grey brain stuck on top, protected by unbreakable clear plasti-glass space helmets.

Their brains have a large bloodshot eye slapped in the middle and a thin cruel mouth underneath. Bristling with weapons, they are completely indestructible.

They're also covered with tacky and utterly tasteless studded jewellery and layers of looped gold chains. Ghastly.

(You might think they want to hide their ugliness by piling on the bling. But then you're not from Galaxy 43b, are you?

They actually want to dazzle their victims by piling on the bling, like the hypnotic eyes of a deadly snake, before they kill them.)

Cosmic cool Captain

The hideously ugly alien still stared silently and threateningly at Harvey. So Harvey coolly stared back. Two could play at that game.

The Bling Bot broke first. 'Hand over the Techno-tium, or we'll blow up your ship,' he growled, his thin lips moving like an open gash in his brain.

Snuffles growled threateningly, his hackles still raised. His huge slobbery lip lifted in a ferocious snarl.

'Down, Snuffles,' ordered Harvey. 'Down and settle.' Reluctantly, and still snarling, the huge Hazard Hunting Hound lay on the deck, protecting Harvey.

Boldly, Harvey carried on: 'What Techno-tium? I don't know what you're talking about,' he bluffed.

'We know you've got it. We've been following you since you took it off the SupaCosmicCargo Delivery Company ship. So give it to us or else . . .' grimaced the Bling Bot. He paused for effect and menacingly clacked his sharp claws with their glittery fake gems. 'Or else we'll blow you and your puny little garbage ship into a gazillion nanocrumbs and plaster you across the entire galaxy.'

Harvey didn't flinch. But he could sense fear creeping round the command bridge and into the crew.

Cosmic clever Captain

Well, Bling Bots might have massive brains, but they not very bright, thought Harvey. So with gobsmacking bravery and brilliant logic, he simply said: 'Is that a good plan?'

'Er . . . yes,' said the Bling Bot, slightly thrown. He'd used his best usual opening threat and it always worked in the past.

'I don't think so,' said Harvey calmly. 'Look, we don't actually have any Techno-tium. But just for fun, let's pretend that we do. OK?'

'Er . . . yes,' said the Bling Bot, now more than

just slightly thrown. His single eye blinked rapidly as if he was struggling to follow Harvey's argument.

'Think about it,' continued Harvey. 'If you blow the *Toxic Spew* into a gazillion nanocrumbs and plaster it across the entire galaxy, then wouldn't you find it a bit difficult to sweep up all the gazillion teeny tiny bits of Techno-tium afterwards?'

'Er . . . yes,' said the Bling Bot. Who obviously hadn't thought of that. And his massive brain flushed pale pink with embarrassment.

'Well, er . . .' he said, his single eye blinking furiously, and sweat breaking out on his brain. 'In that case, you have thirty seconds to hand it over, or we'll smash your shields and board your ship. Then we'll kill you all slowly and painfully and then help ourselves to the Techno-tium. Thirty seconds,' he snarled and bleeped off.

Thirty seconds . . . and counting!

'Grrrr,' growled Snuffles from Harvey's feet.

'What are we going to do?' cried Scrummage.

Harvey was aware of three terrified purple faces with six turquoise eyes staring at him. Yargal was stirring, so to give himself some thinking time, Harvey went over to help haul her up onto her single slimy foot. *Oh, yuk,* he thought, grasping a couple of her slippery tentacles. *She really is disgusting to touch with your bare hands.*

'Captain, we have less than thirty seconds. What are we going to do?' said Maxie urgently.

There was a beat and then Harvey said, 'Hand over the Techno-tium. It's not worth dying for.'

'Noooo!' cried Scrummage. And I mean 'cried'. Like a baby. Tears rolled down his fat cheeks at the thought of just handing over such a valuable cargo.

'Yes!' said Gizmo.

'No!' snapped Maxie. 'Fine captain you're turning out to be. There's no point in just handing it over – they'll kill us anyway. Bling Bots never, ever let anyone go. They'd never live it down. They'll tear us limb from limb, gouge out our eyes, slit our throats, rip out our gizzards and poison our pizza.'

'Oh, Captain,' sobbed Yargal. 'I don't want to be torn limb from limb, and have my eyes gouged out, my throat slit, my gizzards ripped out and my pizza poisoned!'

'Neither do I,' said Harvey. 'Computer, can we outrun them?'

'Nope.'

'Can we outmanoeuvre them?'

'Nope.'

'Can we outshoot them?'

'Nope.'

'Well, what can we do?'

'You have two options,' it said cheerfully. 'You can keep the cargo and be killed. Or you can hand over the cargo and be killed.

'But you have at least ten seconds left to pack in some last-minute fun . . . so go on, let your hair down and party!'

CHAPTER TWENTY

Screaming engines

'Maxie, REVERSE! FULL COSMIC SPEED!'
ordered Harvey. 'Gizmo, do everything you
can to keep the shields up and holding.
Scrummage and Yargal, hold tight!'

'Yes, Captain!' cried Maxie and yanked the
flight control joystick backwards and the *Toxic
Spew* zipped away backwards from the Bling
Bot ship at a fantastic speed.

Harvey nearly flew clean out of the captain's
chair as he was flung forward. (It made a change
from hurtling backwards and smashing his head
against the metal headrest.)

The engines of the *Toxic Spew* screamed in protest – they weren't designed to race backwards at full cosmic speed.

Yargal screamed too – she wasn't designed to race anywhere or anyhow. She wobbled violently and flung her tentacles over her eyes.

Maxie forced the throttle as much as she could, hauling back on the flight joystick with both hands, but within seconds the Bling Bots had caught up. To be fair, they had a much bigger and faster ship.

(It might interest you to know that although the Toxic Spew *has cosmic drive power and a top speed of, oh, lots of gazillion light years per intergalactic hour, the Bling Bot ship has ultra-mega-nova drive power which means it can go faster than the speed of light.*

But of course, you're from Earth so you're probably not that interested in the finer details of spaceship technology, are you?

And even if you were, you probably wouldn't understand them.)

Crazy plan

'Captain, we can't possibly outrun them,' said Gizmo. 'What's your plan?'

'Head back into the interstellar scrapyard and see if we can lose them.'

'Are you crazy? You'll get us all killed!' cried Gizmo.

'We're all going to die!' whimpered Yargal.

'No we're not,' said Harvey. 'They might be bigger and faster, but we're smaller, zippier and we've got one thing they haven't.'

'What's that?'

'The best pilot in the entire Known Universe, and Beyond,' said Harvey. Maxie flashed him a quick grin from under her long fringe.

Harvey was relying on Maxie's expert flying skills to weave her way through the multiple abandoned spacecraft like a star striker chasing a hat trick. He was sure the Bling Bots wouldn't be able to keep up with them.

But then he's new to the job. So hey, what does he know?

Hit and miss

The plucky little *Toxic Spew* (and her equally plucky little crew) plunged into a terrifying cat-and-mouse chase at full pelt, pursued relentlessly by the Bling Bots. Maxie had been right. They would never let them go.

ZAP! ZAP! ZAP!

Their deadly ray guns blazed, pounding the shields of the little garbage control ship whenever they got the chance.

ZAP! ZAP! ZAP!

KA-BOOM!

'Hit!' cried the computer helpfully.

ZAP! ZAP! ZAP!

'Miss . . .'

ZAP–A-ZAP-A-ZAP!

'Miss . . .'

ZAP! ZAP-A-ZAP! ZAP!

KA-BOOM!

'Oh! Hit . . .'

ZAP! ZAP!

KA-KA-KABOOM!

'And another hit!'
'Computer, shut up! ordered Harvey.
The tension on the bridge was unbearable.
Maxie's hands flew over the controls and all
the others could do was watch through the
vision screens in horror as ship after ship
loomed up at them at terrifying speed.

ZIIIIP!

The *Toxic Spew* shot around the back of a derelict Number 26D starport orbital shuttle bus.

DART!

They whizzed underneath an ancient and now decrepit luxury space yacht.

WHOOSH!

They zoomed between an enormous rusting stargate cruiser on the left, and the smashed-up remains of a triple-decker interworld space plane on the right.

But Maxie couldn't shake off the pirate ship. Frankly it was a miracle she didn't kill them all before the Bling Bots got a chance to.

'Harvey, I can't keep this up much longer!' she wailed, her hands whizzing round the controls and her eyes glued to the vision screen. 'Seriously, what are we going to do?'

'Hide,' said Harvey simply.

'What?' cried the crew.

'Hide. They'll think we've got away and they'll give up. Then we'll wait a while, and slip out when they're not looking.'

Hide-and-seek

If you'd slapped the crew round the face with a soggy brown banana skin they wouldn't have been more stunned. In all their multiple intergalactic missions no one had ever suggested something so surprising and simple, so clever and cunning, so inspired and imaginative, as hiding.

(But then, the previous captains of the Toxic Spew *had been a pretty dire bunch. And if any of them had suggested hiding, it wouldn't have been part of a cunning, brave master plan. It would have just been basic cowardice.)*

'Captain, that's brilliant!' exclaimed Gizmo.

Frantically the crew peered through the vision screens looking for a good hiding place among the abandoned spaceships.

'Maxie!' yelled Scrummage, pointing excitedly to a huge ancient space ark up ahead. 'There . . . look, pull in under there.'

So Maxie yanked on the controls, performed a perfect figure-of-eight supersonic handbrake turn and expertly tucked the little garbage ship inside the huge landing cradle of the ancient space ark.

'Computer, cut all power so they can't pick us up on their scanners,' ordered Harvey.

'All power?' questioned the computer bleeping into life.

'Yes,' barked Harvey.

'What even the galley fridge and the toilet flushers?'

'Yes,' snapped Harvey. 'And hurry.'

'Well, all right, but don't blame me if the mozzarella goes mouldy and the loos get blocked.'

The computer cut power and the *Toxic Spew*

was instantly plunged into gloom. The entire bridge was only lit by the tiny little green battery-warning lights on the computer console.

It was dead eerie.

It was dead quiet.

It was dead scary.

It was dead dangerous.

You could have heard a pin drop.

(Well, if Yargal and Snuffles had stopped whimpering you could, and if anyone had dropped a pin.)

I don't think I can describe the terrified tension on the bridge as the enormous Bling Bot ship swept past them, silent and deadly. Its trashy fake diamonds glittering like fish scales on a killer shark. The crew sat frozen with terror, hardly daring to breathe.

And I definitely can't describe the dreadful horror of the moment when, a few seconds later, the pirate ship reversed slowly back, silent and deadly, completely trapping the *Toxic Spew* inside the landing cradle of the ancient space ark.

There was literally no escape.

Uh, oh! thought Harvey. *That wasn't supposed to happen. I think we're all going to die.*

CHAPTER TWENTY-ONE

A horrible, horrible blunder

'We're all going to die!' screamed Yargal, who was pretty sure about the fact.

'We're trapped!' cried Gizmo.

'Flickering chunder!' spluttered Scrummage.

'Fine captain you're turning out to be!' exclaimed Maxie.

Yargal burst into tears. Strings of snotty grey slime snorted out of her like grubby molten mozzarella.

Harvey slumped in the captain's chair on the dimly lit command bridge in utter despair. He'd made a real blunder. A horrible, horrible blunder.

And now his entire crew were going to die. And so was he.

Gutted

Up until now he'd always thought that one day, the crew would be able to get him home. And to the exact moment in time that he'd left, so his mum and dad wouldn't even know he'd been away. But now he wasn't going to get home – at all. Ever. His mum and dad would be gutted.

And then he realised the crew probably all had family too. And friends. And they'd all be gutted too if any, or more probably, all of the crew died. He put his head in his hands, horrified at the full impact of what he'd done.

Just in case he hadn't got his head around who was to blame, the crew instantly launched into a quick-fire game of 'It's all your fault!'.

(I'm not sure if you play this on Earth, so I'll

explain the rules.

It's a ruthless, no-holds-barred shouting game and the aim is to find as many different ways as possible to tell someone: 'It's all your fault'.

The winner is the one who finally makes the victim either storm off in a huff or break down and cry.

It's also known as 'Kick 'em when they're down.')

It doesn't really matter who said what but the first round went something like this:

'You sent us into a trap, why? WHY?'

'What were you thinking?'

'I'm too young to die!'

'Just how stupid are you?'

'How were we supposed to get out?'

'You're the worst captain we've ever had!'

'We're all going to die, and it's *all your fault*!'

The painful and continual barrage only stopped when the ship-to-ship SpaceTime icon on the engineering desk blipped insistently.

Defeated and doomed

Without waiting for Harvey's command, Gizmo ordered the computer to restore power. Then he clicked to accept the connection. And the image of the horribly ugly and now horribly smug Bling Bot filled the vision screen again.

Snuffles' hackles rose and his slathering lips twitched into a silent snarl showing his shark-like teeth.

'Captain,' growled the Bling Bot. 'You're pinned down and you've got no options. So hand over the Techno-tium like a good boy, and we'll kill you quickly and painlessly . . . rather than slowly and agonisingly.' His thin mouth twisted into a grimace that was meant to be a smile.

A low growl rumbled up from deep inside the belly of the huge Hazard Hunting Hound.

'Quiet, Snuffles,' said Harvey softly and sighed. He didn't seem to have any options. He could feel three pairs of bright turquoise eyes, and three yellow googly ones, staring at him in despair. They'd lost. The *Toxic Spew* and her plucky little Bin Men were defeated. Defeated and doomed.

They think it's all over, he thought miserably, *and it probably is.* But then suddenly, in the back of his mind he heard the All Stars coach saying what he always said when the match was going badly: 'It's not over, 'til it's over.'

(I hope this means more to you than it does to me.

Frankly, I'm hoping it means more to Harvey too.)

Harvey pulled himself together. *This is a classic coaching moment,* he told himself. *If you're outclassed by the other team, you don't panic. You tighten your defence, look for every chance, and make your opponents work for every ball.*

So Harvey looked the Bling Bot square in the eye (he only had the one, of course) and said boldly: 'If you want it, come and get it.'

Fluttering upchuck!

GASP, GASP, GASP!

A wave of loud panic-stricken gasps echoed round the command bridge, but Harvey ignored them. He'd had an inspired idea.

'We will lower our shields and you can transport directly into the cargo hold,' he said. 'Shields down, Officer Gizmo, and cut the ship-to-ship SpaceTime link.'

'What?' Cried Gizmo.

'Shields down! And that's an order,' barked Harvey, and Gizmo obeyed.

(I hate to interrupt at this thrilling moment, but is it me, or is he utterly bonkers?

I mean, I know he's from Earth and doesn't have that much experience of ruthless space pirates. But surely even he can grasp that there is nothing worse than a cargo hold full of brutally vicious Bling Bots.)

There was a horrified silence on the bridge of the *Toxic Spew* as the brave Bin Men realised that there was now absolutely nothing standing between them and a bunch of brutally vicious Bling Bots.

The silence was broken by Scrummage. 'Fluttering upchuck, Captain,' he said quietly. 'What have you done?'

CHAPTER TWENTY-TWO

Bling Bots in the cargo hold

Harvey and the crew watched through the cargo webcam as the Bling Bots appeared in the hold. Harvey counted about eight or nine of them. Before their wobbly forms had even finished transporting, their claws clacked excitedly at each other as they fought to get to the valuable cargo first.

'My Techno-tium!' groaned Scrummage with his balding head in his hands.

'Don't worry, Scrummage,' said Harvey, slapping him on the back. 'I have a plan.' And grinning broadly he turned to Gizmo and said:

'Shields up and lock cargo doors!'

And he trapped the Bling Bots in the cargo hold!

(Um . . . actually, can I just ask you something?

If the Bling Bots have got the Toxic Spew *trapped inside the landing cradle of an ancient space ark, and Harvey's got the Bling Bots trapped in the cargo hold of the* Toxic Spew . . .

Then . . . er . . . who's winning?)

'Captain, that was brilliant!' exclaimed Gizmo.

'Awesome,' said Scrummage.

'Actually, you're turning out to be quite a good captain after all,' grinned Maxie. Harvey grinned back.

Garbage men, not pirates

'May I suggest we simply open the cargo hold hatch and let the Bling Bots tumble out and drift off harmlessly into outer space!' said

Gizmo, going over to the garbage control desk and reaching for the hatch lever.

'NOOOOO!' cried Scrummage, shoving him away. 'We'll loose all the Techno-tium too.'

'Who cares?' cried Gizmo, shoving him back and making a grab for the lever again.

'I do!' yelled Scrummage, shoving Gizmo sharply in the chest and snatching hold of the lever.

Gizmo was just about to launch himself full whack at Scrummage when Harvey cut in.

'Gentlemen,' he said firmly. 'Leave the lever alone and stand down.'

'But, Harvey,' cried Maxie. 'It's us or the Bling Bots!'

'If we pull that lever, the Bling Bots will die,' said Harvey.

'Exactly! cried Maxie.

'Again, who cares?' said Gizmo.

'I do,' said Harvey. 'Officer Gizmo, may I remind you we're garbage men not ruthless pirates? I say we hand them over to the Intergalactic Traffic Police and let them deal with them. We'll just keep them in the cargo hold until they arrive.'

Which seemed like a good idea.

But then he's new to the job. So hey, what does he know?

Panic on the command bridge

So Gizmo sat at the engineering desk sending an urgent message to the Intergalactic Traffic Police but before he could even hit 'send' . . .

GASP, GASP, GASP!

A wave of panic-stricken gasps echoed round the command bridge, again.

'Er, Gizmo, you might want to mark that message: "Super Urgent, Read Immediately, Do Not Delay, Top Priority, Deadly Important, Matter of Life and Death"!' cried Maxie, looking at the cargo cam monitor in horror.

Because as soon as the Bling Bots realised

they were trapped in the hold, they turned their multiple deadly weapons on the cargo doors and let rip.

BLAM! BLAM! BLAM!

ZAP! ZAP! ZAP!

(You might be wondering how come the Bling Bots had so many guns with them when, technically, they weren't expecting a fight.

It's because Bling Bots always expect a fight.

Because they're always starting them.)

BLAM! BLAM! BLAM!

ZAP! ZAP-A-ZAP!

GASP, GASP, GASP!

A third wave of panic-stricken gasps echoed around the bridge as they watched the all-out assault on the doors via the webcam.

'Computer,' barked Harvey. 'How much of that can the cargo doors take?'

'I have absolutely no idea,' it said, bleeping cheerfully. 'Hang on, I'll do the sums . . .'

BLEEP, BLIBBLE, BLEEP!

A series of incredibly long numbers, symbols and 3D shapes flashed onto the monitor and scrolled up at incredible speed. Actually, it had nothing to do with the sums. It was just the computer pretending to be clever.

BLAM! BLAM! BLAM!

ZAP! ZAP-A-ZAP!

BLIBBLE . . . BLEEP . . .

'Hurry up!' said Harvey.

'Don't rush me, do you want me to make a mistake? Sometimes I don't think you realise how tricky these sums are,' snapped the computer.

'Now, where was I? Take away six, er . . . or should that be *add* six . . . never mind, I'll just carry it over . . .' it muttered.

Then finally it said, 'Well, I still have absolutely no idea.

'But I'd guess: there's not much time before those ruthless bloodthirsty pirates blast their way through the cargo hold doors, hunt you down mercilessly and slaughter you all.

'You might want to pick up a few things from the weapons store and get down there. Just a thought,' it said casually and bleeped off.

To the galley!

'Scrummage and Gizmo, come with me,' ordered Harvey. 'Maxie and Yargal, barricade yourselves in the galley and take Snuffles to protect you.'

'But I want to fight,' said Maxie.

'But I want you to go to the galley,' said Harvey.

'What, because I'm a girl?'

Harvey thought for a moment. *No*, he thought, *because I actually like you and I don't want you to die.* But he couldn't say that out loud so he said:

'No, because you're the pilot. If anything happens to you, there's no one to fly the ship. So I need you to go to the galley.'

'No, you need all the firepower we've got. Yargal should go to the galley with Snuffles, because she's no good in a fight. But I am and I'm coming with you.' And she pushed her sleeves up her arms and gave him her most challenging stare.

Harvey recognised that look. It was the one the girls in his class used when they weren't going to be pushed around by any of the boys. And he knew better than to ignore it.

'OK,' he said. 'Let's go.'

The crew lost no time in grabbing *all* the ship's weapons and racing down to the cargo hold. By the time they arrived the giant doors were shuddering violently and rattling in their slots.

BLAM! BLAM! BLAM!

ZAP-A-ZAP-A-ZAP!

P'TOING, P'TOING!

(Actually, I've just realised it might help you picture the scene if I tell you what the cargo hold doors look like.

They're huge yellow metal ones that look like they have a massive clunky zip down the middle. They're normally flat and a bit scratched here and there.

But just right now they're full of huge dents and bulges, jagged-edged rips and laser slashes from the Bling Bots' weapons.)

Bazukas, bombs and blasters

'They're not going to hold much longer, sir,'

cried Gizmo, loading his NovaBazuka Mark 3.

'We'll have to go in,' yelled Scrummage, shouldering the ship's huge Jellyfier bomb launcher. Maxie had already loaded her Meteor-Storm pellet gun and was cranking it up to FULL PELT and MAXIMUM STING.

'Stand by to open the doors,' cried Harvey, priming his AstroForce blaster crossbow. 'Now!' he yelled.

Gizmo punched the entry control panel and the huge solid metal doors to the cargo hold of the *Toxic Spew* slid back.

They were met by a hail of fire.

BLAM! BLAM! BLAM!

ZAP-A-ZAP ZAP!

P'TOING, P'TOING!

CHAPTER TWENTY-THREE

All guns blazing

'ATTAAAAAAACK !' yelled Harvey.

Fearlessly, the Bin Men of the *Toxic Spew* charged into the cargo hold with all guns blazing.

ZING, ZING, ZING, ZING!

SPLAT!

PING, PING, PING, PING!

SQUIIIIIIIIRT!

The Bling Bots just laughed and shot back.

P'TOING, P'TOING!

Harvey threw himself to the deck to escape a pounding from a Heavi-Metal rivet and ray gun. He lay on his belly and fired straight back with his AstroForce blaster crossbow.

SQUIIIIIIIIRT!

ZAP-A-ZAP-A-ZAP!

A Sting-Stun zapper smacked Maxie on the elbow and gave her a dead arm, but she just grabbed her Meteor-Storm pellet gun with her other hand and kept on firing:

PING, PING, PING, PING!

ZIP, ZIP, ZIP, ZIP, ZIP!

A direct hit from a shoulder-mounted NuroBlaster knocked Scrummage's legs from under him and he crashed to the ground.

OOOMPH!

Ouch, thought Harvey, *that's got to hurt.* But Scrummage scrambled to his feet and launched a Jellyfier bomb back at his attacker.

SPLAT!

BLAM! BLAM! BLAM!

The supercharged beam from a Disintegrator Ray walloped Gizmo full in the chest and winded him. But he bravely kept firing his NovaBazuka Mark 3.

ZING, ZING, ZING, ZING!

Outgunned and outnumbered

Harvey was astounded by the bravery of his crew. They gave it their best, and more. But they were outgunned and their weapons were useless.

The Jellyfier bombs just slid off the Bling Bots' plasti-glass helmets. Gizmo's NovaBazuka Mark 3 couldn't break through their metal exoskeletons, and the pellets from Maxie's Meteor-Storm pellet gun just boinged back and hit the crew.

'RETREAT!' yelled Harvey, and throwing himself between his crew and the Bling Bots he let rip with his AstroForce blaster crossbow, desperately trying to give them enough cover to get back through the doors.

SQUIIIRRRRRT!

'Close the doors,' he yelled, and the huge metal doors began to slide shut. He made a dash for the gap and just managed to dive

through before they clanged shut. Frantically, he locked the doors.

Then, sweaty and panting, he joined his crew in a collapsed heap on the deck. No one spoke. They were too busy recovering and thanking their lucky cosmic stars they were still alive.

Doomed and done for

BLAM! BLAM! BLAM!

The Bling Bots started on the doors again. The thick metal began to crumple and buckle. The horrified crew realised it was only a matter of minutes before they disintegrated altogether, leaving them at the mercy of the Bling Bots.

(Except of course, Bling Bots have no mercy. They don't see the point.

Actually, can I just say that I was wrong in Chapter Twenty-One? There is something worse than having a bunch of brutally vicious Bling

Bots in your cargo hold.

It's having a bunch of brutally vicious Bling Bots in your cargo hold, trying to get out.)

CHAPTER TWENTY-FOUR

No chance

'It's hopeless,' puffed Scrummage as Harvey helped haul him to his feet.

'We're outnumbered and outgunned,' wheezed Gizmo bent over double.

BLAM! BLAM! BLAM!

P'TOING! P'TOING!

The Bling Bots relentlessly continued pounding the cargo doors.

'Our weapons are rubbish!' panted Maxie.

'No they're not!' snapped Gizmo, who was responsible for supplying all the kit on the ship.

Harvey held up his AstroForce blaster crossbow. 'Be honest, Gizmo. This is a water pistol, isn't it?'

'Er . . . yes.'

'Oh, for crying out loud!' said Maxie.

BLAM! BLAM! BLAM!

P'TOING! P'TOING!

went the Bling Bots' guns.

CRUMPLE, BUCKLE, BUCKLE!

went the doors.

'We have to penetrate their defence,' said Harvey. 'Find their weak spot'.

'But they don't have one,' said Maxie.

'We need something that can rupture their metal exoskeletons and fuse their intricate robotic inner parts,' said Gizmo.

'Huh?' said Scrummage.

'We need something that can get through their metal bodies and gum up their works,' explained Harvey.

P'TOING! P'TOING!

BLAM! BLAM! BLAM!

went the Bling Bots' guns – again.

BUCKLE, BUCKLE!

CRUMBLE, CRUMBLE, RIIIP!

went the doors.

Extra mozzarella!

Suddenly Harvey snatched up his water pistol, er . . . I mean his AstroForce blaster crossbow and pelted off along the corridor. 'Grab your weapons! Follow me.'

'Is this a tactical withdrawal?' panted Gizmo as they pelted along.

'No, I've had an idea.'

Harvey led the crew along the grimy, dimly lit corridors of the *Toxic Spew* to the galley. Their feet squelching softly at every sticky step.

Yargal had barricaded herself and Snuffles behind a heap of old pizza boxes in the galley doorway, and it took a few moments to break in. Snuffles barked and scrabbled furiously and they could hear Yargal whimpering.

AROOOO, AROOOO, AROOOO!

WHIMPER, WHIMPER!

'Don't panic, it's us,' cried Harvey. Then while everyone hurled empty pizza boxes out of the way he astonished them by yelling: 'Yargal, heat up a couple of buckets of your molten mozzarella and bright green glow-in the-dark extra hot spicy rocket fuel sauce.'

Yargal was utterly confused. 'Er . . . yes, sir, if you say so, sir,' she said, then added, 'Um, do you want anything with that?'

'Yup – extra mozzarella!'

Meanwhile, back outside the cargo hold . . .

ZAP-A-ZAP-A-ZAP!

BLAM! BLAM! BLAM!

RIIIIIP! KERRRRANG!

The massive solid metal doors couldn't take any more. They burst open and the Bling Bots stormed through.

Melting mozzarella!

In the galley the crew waited feverishly for the

mozzarella to melt into the rocket fuel sauce.

'Hurry up,' said Scrummage to Yargal, who was frantically stirring the sauce with all of her six tentacles at the same time.

'I'm going as fast as I can,' she whimpered.

Bleep, blibble bleep, the computer's voice broke the tension. 'I hate to interrupt the pizza party,' it said. 'But I thought you might like to know that the cargo doors have given way and the Bling Bots are happily playing hide-and-seek. They're the seekers and they're looking for you.

'But don't worry, they're quite cold. They're searching the bridge. So there's every chance you'll get to have at least a couple of bites of pizza before they track you down and kill you. Enjoy your pizza!' it said cheerily, and bleeped off.

'It's nearly ready,' cried Yargal, frantically beating the sauce.

'We'll take it as it is,' ordered Harvey.

Rocket fuel sauce

Feverishly the crew filled their weapons.

Harvey's AstroForce blaster crossbow and Gizmo's NovaBazuka Mark 3 loaded quickly and easily. Scrummage's huge Jellyfier bomb launcher was slower, but it took litres of the stuff.

They couldn't find a way to pour it into Maxie's Meteor-Storm pellet gun without it trickling out again. So Yargal offered her some sugar-coated cupcake silver balls instead.

'Anything's better than nothing,' said Maxie bravely.

'What are we going to do if it doesn't work?' said Scrummage, shouldering the huge Jellyfier launcher.

'It will,' snapped Maxie, loading her Meteor-Storm pellet gun with silver cupcake sugar balls.

'Harvey's got us through stacks of deadly dangerous situations. Like poisonous killer maggots, a multiple spacecraft pile-up, and exploding garbage. And I bet before he joined us, he probably faced all sorts of other dire and dreadful challenges and he obviously coped with them or he wouldn't be here now,' she said. 'I trust him.'

Harvey was about to remind her that it was his fault they were trapped with the Bling Bots in the first place. But the computer chipped in.

'Oohhh, they're getting much warmer now . . . in fact they're almost getting hot!'

Gizmo turned to Scrummage. 'Maxie's right. Captain Harvey is brilliant! And may I also remind you just how much damage the smallest mini, micro, milli-atom of molten mozzarella can do!'

'And you've no idea how much damage Yargal's bright green glow-in-the-dark extra hot spicy rocket fuel sauce can do either!' said Harvey. 'No offence, Yargal,' he added.

But Yargal was much too terrified to care. She trembled violently from the tips of her yellow googly eyes to the ends of her blue tentacles.

Hold your fire!

They could hear the metal feet of the Bling Bots clanking up the corridors and closing in on them.

'Snuffles, look after Yargal,' ordered Harvey. The huge Hazard Hunting Hound put his enormous shaggy body in front of Yargal, hackles raised, teeth bared, saliva drooling into pools on the floor, snarling and growling ferociously.

'Good boy,' said Harvey.

'Ooooh, they're getting hotter! Hotter, hotter, hotter! Yup, they've found you!' cried the computer gaily as the clank of robotic feet got nearer and nearer.

'Computer, SHUT UP!' barked Harvey.

'Oh, sorreee, I was only trying to add a little party spirit.'

The Bling Bots were just outside the galley door.

'Take up positions and standby,' cried Harvey. The crew levelled their guns at the galley doorway. 'Hold your fire. Steady, steady . . . wait for my command.

'They think it's all over . . .' muttered Harvey to himself through clenched teeth, and as the galley door flung open and the Bling Bots stormed in he added, 'it is now!'

'FIRE!' he yelled.

And the brave but grubby Bin Men let rip with all guns blazing, or rather squirting.

SQUIIIIIIIRT! SPLAT!

BLAM! BLAM! BLAM!

SQUIIIIIIIRT, SPLAT! SPLATTER, SPLAT!

ZAP-A-ZAP-A-ZAP!

P'TOING! P'TOING!

SQUIIIIIIIRT, SPLATTER, SPLATTER, SQUIIIIIIIRT,

SPLAT!

Then suddenly,

BZZZZ BZZ BZZZZZZ!

There was a wonderful buzzing sound –

BZZZZ TZZCHHER ZTTZZZZ BZZ!

exactly as if some electrical wires were touching each other when they shouldn't be, and the Bling Bots stopped shooting. Their huge single eyes rolled shut in their brains, and their robotic bodies clunked and wound down, like remote control toys when the batteries die.

It was all over.

The Bling Bots didn't stand a chance against Yargal's molten mozzarella and bright green glow-in the-dark extra hot spicy rocket fuel sauce.

(But then, hey, who does?)

CHAPTER TWENTY-FIVE

Splattered mozzarella!

Harvey and Maxie sat slumped and exhausted on the filthy deck in the galley of the *Toxic Spew*. The entire room was splattered with a staggering quantity of molten mozzarella and rocket fuel sauce.

Snuffles was having the time of his life, licking up endless dollops of sauce with his huge tongue.

Blobs of it dripped off the surfaces and dribbled down the fridge. The hot plates were plastered with it, and splodges of molten mozzarella were smeared all over the 3D pizza printer.

In all honesty it didn't look that much different than usual.

(Sorry, were you imagining that the Toxic Spew *would have a squeaky clean galley with spotless metal surfaces and gleaming state-of-the-art cooking equipment?*

Don't be silly.)

The Bling Bots were gummed up, tied up and locked up in Yargal's large food storage bins. Gizmo had gone to the bridge to alert the Intergalactic Traffic Police.

Yargal was frantically searching through cupboards and wondering if she could rustle up a celebratory pizza.

But she couldn't find any mozzarella.

Of course there was plenty of it splattered all over the galley. But even Yargal has some standards.

How much Techno-tium!?

It won't surprise you to know that Scrummage had dashed off to the cargo hold to see how much Techno-tium they had – and more importantly, how much it was worth. Maxie and Harvey were too tired to care.

Harvey sat cross-legged and weary with his head in his hands. 'I nearly got us all killed,' he said to Maxie quietly.

'It wasn't your fault,' she said.

'Yes it was. It was my idea to hide – and then I got us trapped.'

Maxie tucked her hair behind her ears and then said firmly. 'Harvey, it was *our* fault. And I'm not just saying that to make you feel better.

'You didn't know how dangerous it was having such valuable cargo. But we did. And we knew that if we told you, you wouldn't let us take the risk. So we didn't tell you,' she shrugged.

'And anyhow, if it wasn't for you we wouldn't have got away with it. But we did . . . and now we're going to be rich!' She laughed, her bright turquoise eyes shining in her purple face. 'RICH!'

Just at that moment Scrummage hailed them on the inter-ship coms SpaceTime system from the cargo hold. His voice sounded strangely tense.

'I'm holding the Techno-tium,' he said.

'How much is there?' asked Maxie breathlessly.

There was a pause while Scrummage seemed to be struggling to control his emotions, and then he said: 'It's about the size of a silver cupcake sugar ball.'

'What! Is that all?'

'Yup,' said Scrummage. He was gutted.

'Computer, how much is that worth?' asked Harvey.

The computer was just about to answer, but Gizmo cut in . . .

'Bridge to Captain, the Intergalactic Traffic Police are on their way. Um . . . do we know how much Techno-tium we have yet?' he added, trying to sound casual. 'And, more importantly, what it's worth!'

'Er, yes,' said Harvey.

'I was just about to say when you so rudely interrupted me,' snipped the computer.

But Gizmo was too excited to bother about manners. 'Well?' he blurted out eagerly. 'Is there enough for a new Cygnus 7 single-seater shuttle craft with its revolutionary TripTronic gearing system?'

'Nope,' said the computer.

'Oh,' said Gizmo flatly.

'Is there enough for a personal 3D pizza printer, unlimited supplies of mozzarella, chocolate, banana custard and chilli sauce, and a small planet with sandy white beaches and a heated sea?' asked Scrummage hopefully.

'Nope!'

'Speckled vomit!' sighed Scrummage disappointedly.

'How about a Cassini Personal HeliDroid, with inbuilt VidiScape gaming system, subsonic sound, 3V-360 VisionVisor, multi-player, multi-platform and multi-universe enabled features, downloadable cosmic content capability, pangalactic performance power enhancers and the Stella BonusBox? asked Maxie.

'Nope!'

'Which means there's nowhere near enough for us to give up garbage collecting long enough to find Earth,' said Harvey, sadly.

'Absolutely correct!' said the computer. 'But I'm glad you mentioned that. Because I think I've found your home planet!'

'Really!' cried Harvey excitedly.

'Is this Earth?'

'Is it purple with a pink gas cloud ring, orbited by three glow-in-the-dark lime green moons just the other side of the asteroid belt in the Erical Galaxy?'

'Nope,' said Harvey.

'Ah. In that case I haven't. Sorry. Never mind,

cheer up! Because there *is* enough Techno-tium to buy a rubber counter gravity bumper, a reactor-driven heat shield, and a reversing camera for the ship! Well, second-hand ones off the Outernet.'

'Oh, excellent!' cried Gizmo.

'Cool!' said Maxie, who was fed up with reversing the *Toxic Spew* and not being able to see what she was doing.

'And, as well as getting the vital spare parts for the ship, there's enough Techno-tium to get everyone a bumper family-size pack of grated mozzarella cheese – each!'

'Well, I guess that's better than nothing,' said Harvey.

But then he's new to the job. So hey, what does he know!

ACKNOWLEDGEMENTS

With the most enormous and heartfelt thanks to:

Gaia Banks for continuing to give me most excellent, and honest, criticism as well as support and advice and some rather nice lunches.

Sara O'Connor for her skilful editing and story guidance, and the fabulous Hot Key Books team, especially Jenny Jacoby and Megan Farr.

Cait Davies from Hot Key Books for her tireless efforts to turn me from technodork to technotyro – a remarkable achievement.

Jacqueline Wilson for encouraging me and saying such lovely things about the first Harvey Drew book.

Alfie, Bertie, Archie and Annie Beth for being proud of me.

And Annie Beth for giving Maxie the best line in the

book: 'Death by pizza! Not a very *heroic* way to die!'

And finally,

Sam Hearn for his brilliant illustrations. Sam, this is a huge thank you for adding so much in your pictures. Sam, you rock.

CAS LESTER

Cas spent many years having a fabulous time, and a great deal of fun, working in children's television drama with CBBC. She developed and executive-produced lots of programmes including JACKANORY, MUDDLE EARTH, THE MAGICIAN OF SAMARKAND, BIG KIDS and THE STORY OF TRACY BEAKER. Her programmes have been nominated for numerous awards, including BAFTAS, Royal Television Awards and Broadcast Children's Awards.

Now she's having a fabulous time, and a great deal of fun, writing books for children, helping out in a primary school library and mucking about with her family. She has four children, three chickens and a daft dog called Bramble. She would absolutely love to go into space. But not on the *Toxic Spew.*

FROM THE EXPERT

Professor Matthew Colless is an astronomer who is Director of the Research School of Astronomy and Astrophysics at the Australian National University in Canberra. His main research is on understanding how galaxies and larger structures form in the universe. However, he also helps to build instruments for telescopes, and this has led him to get involved in a new research centre that is working on solutions to the problem of space junk.

Q. What is space trash?
A. Space trash is all the stuff orbiting the Earth that's not meant to be there.

Q. Where does it come from?
A. Wherever people go they leave trash behind, and space is no different. Space trash includes all sorts of things: satellites that no longer work, debris from collisions between satellites, parts off old rockets, tools lost by astronauts, and even just flecks of paint off spacecraft.

Q. How much of it is there?
A. Lots! At present tens of thousands of pieces of space junk are being tracked, but it is estimated that there are several hundred thousand pieces of space junk orbiting the Earth.

Q. Why is it a problem?

A. Space trash is a problem because it can collide with valuable things like communications satellites or the International Space Station and cause serious damage. Even small pieces of space trash can do a lot of damage because things in orbit move so quickly. In low Earth orbit things are moving at about 7 km/s (16000 mph) – or about ten times faster than a bullet!

Q. What are space experts doing about it?

A. The first thing to do is to track the space trash so you know how much there is and where it is, so that satellites and the International Space Station can manoeuvre to avoid it. But some satellites can't do that, so another option is move the space trash instead by pushing it with a laser beam. But if there's too much space junk it won't be possible to dodge or push it out of the way all the time. So we need to figure out ways to reduce the amount of junk in orbit. One way is to use lasers to slow the space junk down so it falls out of orbit and burns up harmlessly in the atmosphere.

Q. What is your project going to do?
A. We are working on all these things: we are trying to improve our ability to find and track space junk; we are figuring out how to predict the orbits more accurately so we know where it will be in future; and we are working on ways to push junk around with lasers. We are using a technique from astronomy called 'adaptive optics' which works a bit like noise-cancelling headphones to remove the blur caused by the atmosphere. That helps us see smaller, fainter, more distant bits of space junk, and to focus laser beams more precisely on things in orbit.

Q. How much is it going to cost?

A. Our program will spend tens of millions of dollars improving our ability to manage space junk, and will use facilities worth about a hundred million dollars (£55million). That's a lot of money, but then the value of all the satellites and spacecraft in orbit is about 900 billion dollars (over £500million) and the value of the services they provide (like GPS, communications, weather forecasting and so on) is trillions of dollars – so it's worth spending a lot to protect them!

LOVE READING? LOVE WRITING?

Check out <u>www.thestoryadventure.com</u>

Where people like you help authors like Cas write books!